Don't Go, Ramanya

RUSH LEAMING

BRIDGEWOOD ENT.

ISBN: 069277288X
ISBN-13: 978-0692772881

SPECIAL THANKS

Blair Lott, and Jane Speight for reading the first draft

Starr Waddell for her expert copyediting as well as her team of beta readers at Quiethouse Editing

Mark Petersen for pointing me East all those years ago

All the people at Wat Prok and Mary Knoll for taking in a lost soul

And finally, to my Chickencake for always making me proud

AUTHOR'S NOTES

<u>Pronunciation tips:</u>

- The honorific "Pra" for a Buddhist monk is also sometimes written as "Phra". I decided to go with the phonetically simpler version
- Our hero's name is pronounced with all short "a" sounds: "Rah-mahn-yah"
- The Mon ("moan") Tribe
- The Karen ("kah-ren") Tribe
- Wat Prok is usually pronounced with a silent "k": ("pro")

<u>Money matters:</u>

In 1999, the exchange rate was 1 Thai baht = $0.03; i.e. 100 baht = $3.00

<u>Historical facts:</u>

As the disclaimer says, this is a work of fiction: everything is true, and at the same time, none of it is true.

However, many of the events in the book did occur, including the hostage crisis at the Myanmar Embassy in Bangkok. Feel free to look them up...

For Ramanya

Part One

Friday, October 1, 1999

Nobody speaks. In the predawn, in a muddy field at the far edge of Bangkok, three men wearing camouflage jumpsuits emerge from behind a wall of bushes. They move in a well-rehearsed rhythm, pointing fingers, nodding heads. A slightly built man with light-brown skin, a taut face, and a slick black pompadour leads them toward a cargo truck that sits alone and nearly invisible. The driver and the young man in the passenger seat leap from the front cab. They roll up the back tailgate to reveal dozens of crates of plastic soda bottles—the red, yellow, and orange colors slightly glowing in the darkness like just-fading fireflies. The passenger opens a large canvas duffle bag; he shines a penlight inside to show the other men five assault rifles, coils of rope, machetes, smoke grenades, and a folded banner. The man with the pompadour takes one of the guns. Two others follow him, and they climb in the back of the truck, sitting down against the far wall. The driver slides the pallets of soda together in a row, shielding the men from sight. A hand trembles, the young passenger's, as he reaches into the bag and pulls out two pairs of blue overalls with the brand name Fanta stitched on front. The driver grabs the young man's hand to steady it and stares hard into his eyes. Breathe in, exhale, breathe in, exhale; then he and the driver put on the clothes and climb back in the front seat. The engine growls to life, ripping through the quiet early morning. The driver steers the truck onto the road and heads toward the heart of the city...

Chapter One

In the darkness, his dead mother's voice stabbed Ramanya in the ears, telling him, "Wake up. We need to speak." Ramanya opened his eyes. At first, everything seemed normal. A dim electric night-light spread thick shadows on the cinder-block walls. He looked around the dormitory to see the other members of his group, six Buddhist monks, lying prone on thin mattresses, sleeping on the floor. The room was cold. White snakes crawled from his mouth and swirled in the air. It was the first time since he had come to this temple, Wat Prok in Bangkok, Thailand, that he had ever seen the temperature drop low enough to cause frosted breath.

His mother's voice continued to circle around the room, telling him, "Up! Up! Please get up!" He looked for any outline or shape of a body but found none. There was no weight to his arms and legs, so he floated out of his bed, his body turning sideways, as he pulled his hands back and forth and swam across the room to the open doorway. Ramanya saw a white cat with pink eyes jump into the air, and he followed as it ran up a narrow, crumbling staircase to an open-air classroom on the top floor of the temple. The jagged city skyline surrounded him. He sat down on the ledge next to the cat while his mother's voice seemed to tumble from the sky.

"I don't see how you live here," she said. "You always hated cities."

He stroked the fur on the back of the cat. "I stay here at the temple most of the time."

"You look thin."

"You always say that."

He heard his mother laugh. "What am I really seeing— you a monk? Shaved head and orange robes? All my life I never once heard you pray."

"Tissa came here with me. We came soon after it happened…" A mechanical sound, a low pounding and humming, began rising in the distance.

"Your sister misses you. So do I."

The cat's tongue, like wet sandpaper, licked the skin between his fingers. Ramanya closed his eyes. "I'm so sorry. If I had only known—"

"But you don't know! That's what I came here to tell you. You left too soon. We—"

A single gunshot cracked open the breastbone of the night. The pounding and humming noise rushed in and filled the air. The floor of the classroom began to shake. The cat raised its head, hissing, as the temple walls quivered, and the chopping, thrashing sound sent the cat running down the staircase. Ramanya reached out his arm to stop it, his mouth open, the muscles in his throat vibrating up and down, but no voice came out, only the pounding, pounding that began to fade and dissipate, dissipate and fade, until the last sound to be heard was a distant car horn on a faraway street. Ramanya slumped to the floor and pulled his robes tighter around his slender body. A chill crawled across his skin while behind him dozens of steel and neon fingers scratched against the violet sky. Above a wall of trees, pushed far against the horizon, the red electric letters of the HSBC building blinked on and off…

On and off…

On and off…

****

When Ramanya woke the second time, it was just shy of four a.m. He was on his mat in the bedroom with his group. His robes lay

12

untouched, carefully folded on the chair next to his bed, just as they had been when he went to sleep. The paper doorway was empty. His breath was invisible. Tissa, his best friend and leader of his group, was asleep next to him, and the electric night-light glowed against the wall.

Ramanya could still feel where the cat's bumpy tongue had rubbed the skin between his fingers—as if it had really happened. He went over the dream again. Just a random mash of images or something more? He couldn't tell, but it didn't matter. Neither of those changed the fact that his mother and the rest of his family in Burma were dead.

The other monks now stirred awake. He rose from his mat and headed to the common toilet next to the stairs. From the courtyard below, he could hear some of the temple dogs barking and whining, and he saw a brown cat rush down the staircase. On the bottom step, there was a forgotten plate of food: chicken bones covered in ants. He threw it in the rubbish bin, but a few of the ants escaped from the dish and crawled along his hand. Ramanya carefully removed them and placed each one back onto the ground where they scurried away. He walked down to the center of the temple to join the other groups now gathering in the *viharn,* the main worship room, for morning prayers. Tissa came up next to him and asked him how he slept. Ramanya, still trying to process it all, simply replied, "Well."

A novice monk lit incense, and a cloud of sandalwood filled the room. They sat on the floor and bowed before their statue of the Buddha. Ramanya took slow, deep breaths and tried clear his mind, but the white cat and other images of the dream kept scratching away inside his head. *Go. Go away.*

His failed meditation came to an end. Pale morning light first cracked from the sky. Ramanya and the other monks gathered their alms bowls to spread out around the surrounding neighborhoods. They took to the streets, barefoot and with robes wrapped snugly across their bodies, to mingle with the outside world—the buzzing, hot, sticky soup of a city of ten million people coming to life. Ramanya went on his usual route: turning right outside the red and gold gates of the temple, walking past the cracked opening of the Chinese cemetery and along Soi 22 toward Silom Road.

The early morning heat was already enough for sweat to form on the back of his neck. His head felt thick and his body heavy like it was moving through a stiff cloud. He walked past all the market stalls springing to life, all the food carts sizzling and steaming with their various delicacies, all the flower vendors, the shopkeepers, and all the school children walking in packs, wearing their white shirts

14

and blue skirts or pants. Several people smiled at him and gently waved him over. They scooped out portions of their own breakfast or a selection of whatever goods they were selling and placed them in his bowl. One of the vendors, a young Thai man wearing a tattered yellow apron, held out a piece of crispy, perfectly roasted golden-brown duck and asked Ramanya if he could accept it. Ramanya said, "Yes," explaining their abbot allowed them to eat meat if it was offered though he could never ask for it and could never, now as a monk, ask someone to kill another living creature. He watched the young man carefully place it in his bowl. Most mornings, when such special gifts were handed to him, he would be thrilled to accept them. Today, he wasn't thrilled.

****

It was while standing outside a 7-Eleven store, waiting for the cashier to reappear with an offering, that Ramanya first felt like someone was watching him. To his left was a beauty salon, still shuttered as it was not yet eight a.m., and beyond it at the edge of Lumphini Park, he could see the soaring statue of King Rama IV, cast as a bronze soldier in a pith helmet, jutting into the cloudless sky. To his right was a Kentucky Fried Chicken, doors open for breakfast. The feeling of being watched came from the right, and leaning beneath the awning of the KFC was a thin, sienna-skinned man with a scar on his chin, wearing a red silk shirt and smoking a cigarette. The man smiled at Ramanya—not unusual, everyone smiled at a monk—but something about him stood out from the rest of the population swarming around this street. He seemed in no hurry—that was what Ramanya thought. Everyone else was hurrying to work or working hard to open their stores, cook their food, or get to school, but this man had no urgency in his limbs. He smoked, exhaling long and slow, and smiled at Ramanya yet again.

The doors of the 7-Eleven opened and the cashier, a young woman Ramanya knew as June—her English nickname—emerged from the store. She handed Ramanya two bottles of water and a few sweet red-bean buns wrapped in cloth paper, being careful to make sure her hands didn't touch his directly.

"*Kam-sa-hamida,* Pra Ramanya," she said. "Thank you. My mother. She's very ill. May I ask you to send good wishes for her? For her recovery or for a peaceful end and a happy renewal?"

"Of course."

June put her hands together in front of her face and gently bowed her head at Ramanya. Together they closed their eyes and sent out thoughts of good health. When Ramanya opened his eyes, he looked toward the KFC. The man in the silk shirt was gone.

June thanked him once again and went back inside the store. With his alms bowl now full and an hour having passed, it was time to return to Wat Prok. The sun was now completely awake, it's blistering rays fully charged, searing the asphalt and concrete of the city. Even after living here sixteen months, having fled the cool mountain villages of his home in Burma (he would never say the name Myanmar) Ramanya's bare feet were still not used to the cracked walkways and heat, curling and wincing as he walked toward home.

Several times Ramanya glanced behind him, still feeling a slight pressure boring into his back as if someone's eyes had latched onto him. He thought he kept seeing the flash of a red shirt following him, but each time he turned around, it would disappear into the crowd. Once, he heard a sharp whistle, and thought he felt someone poke him on his shoulder; but again, as soon as he turned around, no one was there, only a wall of anonymous faces moving through the city.

He pushed open the heavy red and gold gate of the temple and walked toward the *sala*, the temple's dining and meeting hall. It was on the ground floor of their compound, tucked underneath the shade of young banyan tree. Ramanya and all the other monks gathered together at long, wooden benches and each carefully

17

unraveled the offerings of food they had received. Once his meal was finished, he joined the others as they washed out their alms bowls and then the temple children poured in, bouncing around with hungry energy. Ramanya helped Tissa scoop out plates of fish and vegetables for each of the orphans under their care. Some of the monks formed a chain as they carried the food and poured water and juice in plastic cups, while others tried to keep order for the few rambunctious kids who always seemed to cause trouble.

As Ramanya crossed the courtyard, moving toward the eastern wing and his bedroom, another group of children squealed with delight against the wall of the telephone room. Six of them formed a tight semicircle, huddling around a small object that leaped with flashes of white in and out of their legs.

Ramanya approached them. "What are you children doing?"

One young girl spun around, a wide smile splitting her brown face. Then the others parted, and Ramanya saw a skinny albino cat curled against the base of the wall. It had thin pink eyes, and its tongue lashed at its whiskers.

"We found it this morning," the young girl said. "Isn't it pretty?"

Ramanya stared at the cat. The cat ignored him and continued to leap and play, running through the children's legs.

"Can we keep it?" asked the girl.

"Ask Pra Sarawon," said Ramanya. "But I'm sure he will agree... You say you found it this morning?"

"An hour ago. I've never seen a cat with pink eyes," she said.

Ramanya's legs quivered just a bit. "Make sure you ask Pra Sarawon."

"Pra Ramanya!" a strange voice called out.

Ramanya turned, and standing next to the front gate was the man with the red silk shirt. The man gave the traditional *wai* greeting, holding his hands pressed together in front of his face and bowing his head toward Ramanya.

"You are Pra Ramanya?" the man asked as he walked closer toward him.

Ramanya dug his feet deeper into the ground. "I saw you in the city," he said.

"Are you Ramanya, from the village Lamsing?" asked the man.

Ramanya didn't respond.

"Yes, you are. You are the Black Fox. I've found you."

That name, a name not heard for sixteen months, reached inside Ramanya with sharp claws. Survival instinct, drilled into him for so many years, rose up and steadied his face. "I don't know what you are saying," he said. "Is there something I can do for you?"

"I know who you are," said the man, as he lit a cigarette. "You are the bomb-maker."

Ramanya smiled at him. "I'm sorry. You must have me confused with someone else."

"I have a message for you. From your family."

At that moment, Ramanya felt a familiar wet sandpaper sensation digging between his toes. The white cat had crawled over to him and now lay on the ground, licking his feet.

"Did you hear me?" said the man. "I said your family is alive."

Chapter Two

Something was about to happen. Father Bob Hanlan looked out his living room window, stood behind his white curtain, and sucked on a spoonful of peanut butter. His narrow townhouse stood at the end of a short alley, and the early morning activity that scurried in front of him seemed normal—but he wasn't sold on that. There was the ice cream shop—two teenagers sat at a plastic table drinking tall frosted glasses of pink bubble tea. There was the shoe store—the owner was sweeping the pavement in front of the door. And there was the gray three-story apartment building—an elderly woman entered it carrying plastic bags stuffed with jackfruit and mangoes.

Normal.

It had only been three days earlier Bob had seen two men with burnt brown faces hanging around at the end of his alley, leather military cloaks wrapped around their olive pants, sticking out like bruised hangnails on a manicured thumb. They had been milling about with no obvious destination, smoking cigarettes, looking toward his gated, two-story home that stuck out like a hangnail itself on this blue-collar street. Bob had watched them for over an hour, and that hadn't been the only time. In fact, most everywhere Bob went lately, he kept seeing and feeling shadows out of the corner of his eye—slinking, lurking, following. Sometimes he would suddenly turn around, but they would disappear.

Or had they really been there in the first place? He wasn't sure anymore. He looked toward the side of his house then back down the alley. The two teenagers left their now empty glasses on the table and walked away. Maybe those men in the leather cloaks had just been looking for a nice spot in the shade to have a smoke. Maybe everyone had forgotten what Bob did a few weeks ago in Rangoon, and they would all just leave him alone. Maybe Bob just needed to get his aging eyes checked and start wearing glasses. Maybe.

At the end of the alley were the motorcycle taxis run by a group of five teenagers that made about forty quid a day ferrying people up and down the congested streets of Bangkok. Father Bob had been waiting for one of the kids to deliver a message to him. The kid was late. Bob dug into his jar of peanut butter again. He saw a young boy in the alley playing soccer by himself with a ball made from rubber bands and string. He knew his English nickname was Hank, and Bob made a mental note to buy him a proper ball, only one hundred Thai baht at the toy store around the corner. He opened the front door of his home and motioned the boy over to his steps.

"Hank, do me a favor, would you, mate? Scurry up to the main road and see if Tommy is there." He pressed a fifty baht note into the young boy's palm.

"*Kòp kun mâak,* thanks, Poppa Bob," the boy said and bowed his head before sprinting toward the group of motorcycle drivers. He watched the boy splash in and out of large puddles left behind by the recent storms. Thailand was near the end of its rainy season (it seemed to only rain at night) and near the end of *Khao Pansa,* or Buddhist Lent. When the weather cleared, Bob would be on the road more, visiting the various camps and programs around the country that he and his colleagues at Saint Thomas Ministries had established. It was fine by him; he was a restless sort, he always admitted, and he liked to be out in the field rather than sitting at a desk in an office.

A teenage Thai boy, his nickname Tommy, came rushing up on his Honda 150 motorbike, the engine whirring at a high pitch, the little electric horn sounding like a dying goat. Tommy was hip-hop

23

all the way. He had spiky hair, a gold earring, baggy pants, and a Tupac Lives! T-shirt. Father Bob had been to his home in the slums and met his parents and two sisters. His mom worked on the city buses as a ticket taker, and his dad ran a water taxi that moved along the *klongs,* the oil-slicked canals that snaked through the heart of the city. Father Bob had even bought him a Snoop Dogg CD last Christmas.

"It's happening today!" Tommy shouted over the engine.

"Where? When?" Bob shouted back.

"I don't know. That's what I was waiting to find out. Soon I know, I come here."

"All right. As *soon* as you know." Father Bob peeled off three fifty baht notes and held them in front of Tommy. Tommy reached for them, but Bob pulled back. "How are your grades?"

Tommy stuck out his chest and smiled. "Three A's. Only a C in math."

"You need to work on that. You want to be a towering businessman, you need to learn how to count."

"Algebra, Father Bob. Who needs it?"

Bob smiled and pressed the money into Tommy's palm. "You're right. I'm almost fifty years old and have never used it once! Bollocks!"

A wide grin broke across Tommy's face. "Bollocks! Bollocks!" he chanted.

The thin engine kicked up a puff of blue smoke, and Tommy shot back to the intersection of the main road. Father Bob went inside, locked the three deadbolts on his front door, and pulled his curtains tight. He caught a glimpse of himself in the hall mirror and stopped.

Fifty? Right around the corner. He looked at the patches of gray and the streaks of white in his sandy-blond hair. Couldn't say salt and pepper. More like… curry and snow. He liked that. Yes, very good—curry and snow. Still, he felt sharp for his age. He was fit and a trim eighty-five kilos for his six-foot-one frame. When he was younger at Cambridge, he used to box and swim, and he still swam two to three days a week at the sports club near his office. He had lots of energy… perhaps too much. Yes, perhaps too much, indeed. Those shadows he kept seeing. Yes, he might have really done it this time. He might have bitten off much, much more than he could ever possibly chew—and he might be in danger of choking to death.

Bob heard Tommy's motorbike screaming down the alley, its horn bleating nonstop. He unlocked his door and threw it open. Tommy skidded up, splashing through a puddle at the bottom of his steps.

"Now!" shouted Tommy. "It's happening now!"

"Now? Where?" yelled Bob.

"At the embassy. Inside the embassy!"

"*Inside* the embassy?" Bob said, then suddenly realized what it meant. "Oh no. No, no, no... Bloody hell! Take me up there. Now!"

Bob slammed his door shut and hopped on the back of the bike. He wrapped his arms around Tommy's midsection, and they swerved around and blasted out of the alley onto the main road.

The Burmese embassy was about two kilometers away up on Pan Road, and Bob held on tight as Tommy zigged in and out of stopped traffic, sometimes hopping up on medians and sidewalks, swooping around soup carts and flower vendors. He could hear police sirens screaming all around them on the parallel streets. He heard an ambulance come up behind him, and he tugged on Tommy's shoulder to move over and let it pass. The ambulance was heading toward Pan Road.

Father Bob caught a glimpse of the white gates and the gold sign declaring it to be The Embassy of the Union of Myanmar, but before they could reach any closer, a Thai military truck pulled up and blocked the road. Half a dozen soldiers jumped out with rifles drawn and spread out along the walls.

"We'll go around the hospital!" shouted Tommy, and then they turned and headed back toward Saint Louis Hospital. They went around to the emergency entrance where there was a dirt footpath running along the side of the main building, wide enough for Tommy to steer the bike through. They came out at the back wall of the embassy. More sirens sliced through the air, and Father Bob hopped off the bike. On the roof of the embassy, a figure emerged, clad in a camouflage jumpsuit, shaking a machine gun in the air. Another emerged, and together they unfurled a white banner, hand painted with bright-blue letters that said: BURMA NOT MYANMAR! FREEDOM FOR BURMA! DEMOCRACY NOW! They fired their guns into the air, and Father Bob felt all the water get sucked out of his throat and mouth. "Bloody, bloody, bloody, bloody hell," he rasped.

"This is not what you wanted?" asked Tommy.

"No," said Bob. "This is not what I wanted at all."

"It's exciting," said Tommy.

Shouting, screaming, sirens, gunshots, soldiers running, glass breaking: columns of black smoke rose from the courtyard on the other side of the embassy walls that were topped with thick swirls of steel barbed wire. Chaos exploded all around them. Another

Burmese man with a slick black pompadour and a camouflage suit ran onto the roof and jumped up and down. For a short second he froze and looked down into the alley, off the back wall, and straight into Bob's eyes. The man smiled at Bob and nodded then disappeared back inside the building.

Bob rubbed his hands across his face several times. He heard another woman scream from behind the wall. He pulled Tommy and leaped back onto the motorbike. "I need to get away from here. Let's go!"

"Where?" shouted Tommy.

"To the temple. To Wat Prok," said Bob as the sounds of a helicopter pounded overhead.

Chapter Three

Michael Shaw pulled his notebooks and crib sheets and a box of chalk from his backpack as the morning sun crashed through the open-air walls of the classroom. Six Buddhist monks from Burma, sitting upright in their desks, waited for him to begin his lesson.

Present perfect. That's a tricky one. How do you teach the present perfect tense? Michael shuffled around papers and thumbed through his books, trying to buy himself more time. *I have seen. I have been. I have been to Japan. I have seen the latest James Bond movie. James Bond? Do they even know who he is? Have they ever seen a movie? Yes, some of them had. They have a computer, for Christ sakes. They have e-mail and their own website. Don't say Christ. You are in a Buddhist temple. Is that forbidden? I don't know…*

Dragonflies danced in his gut. He told himself that meant he cared about what he did, that he wanted to do a good job. And he always did do a good job. Once he got into the swing of things. Once the flapping bugs exhausted themselves and left him alone. He liked coming here and teaching the monks. He liked slipping off his shoes and roaming around the room barefoot, scratching examples of grammar on the chalkboard. Their English was good. This was an advanced class, and he had been surprised at that fact when Father Bob hired him for this job three months ago. Well, it wasn't quite a real job. He didn't get paid. Bob did set him up with a free apartment as part of the deal, decent, with air conditioning, just a ten-minute walk from the temple. The stroll to Wat Prok every morning, and the hour he spent here with these seven Buddhist monks—*wait, there's only six today. Who's missing?*—was his favorite part of each day. The rest usually went downhill.

"Where's Ramanya?" Michael asked in a rumbling, not-quite-awake, baritone voice.

Pra Tissa, the leader of the group, and Michael's second-favorite student after Pra Ramanya, raised his hand.

"Yes, Tissa?"

"I'm sorry, teacher. But Pra Ramanya isn't feeling well today. He is in his room."

"Is there anything I can do? Should I call Father Bob?"

"I ask him that as well and he refused. He said he will just rest."

"Ok. But the correct form is *asked*. I *asked* him that as well. Past simple tense."

"Yes, teacher. Please forgive me," said Tissa.

Michael smiled. How could you not like these guys? "It's ok. You don't need to apologize every time you make a mistake. Remember, making mistakes is good. Making mistakes is how you learn."

"Yes, teacher. Forgive me again. I shall apologize less."

Present perfect exploded out of Michael like candy from a piñata. He bounded around the room, with the sprawling Bangkok skyline behind him, and had them work in pairs, interviewing each other, giving each a list of questions designed to practice this tense that most languages in the world had no use for. *Have you ever flown in an airplane? Yes, I have flown in an airplane.* Then he threw them a curveball, which they all caught beautifully. They had to expand their answers by also using the past simple. This was to show them the difference between the two. *Have you ever been to the beach? Yes, I have been to the beach. I went there last summer.*

Oh, they got it. These guys were good, very sharp. Michael

31

was good too. He was on fire today, a true solar flare of grammar and syntax, filling each of these monks with his own cosmic ball of wit and enlightenment. They laughed. They had a great time. And about fifteen minutes before the end of class, Ramanya showed up, bowing his head in sincere shame and apologies.

"It's fine," said Michael, energy and sunshine oozing from every pore of his skin. This is what rock stars must feel like. Or actors in a hit Broadway play. "I can work with you later one-on-one if you like and get you up to speed. Does everyone remember that idiom: *to get one up to speed?* We studied it a few weeks ago."

Pra Nanda, one of the quieter ones of the group, raised his hand. "It means to help someone become aware of the latest information."

"Excellent! I tell you, you all are wonderful students. Just wonderful. I really love coming here each morning."

"We love having you come as well," said Ramanya. "You help us so much."

A big sticky love fest was what they were all swimming in. Cotton candy. Plum pie.

As class ended, Michael was still buzzing. His vision was sharp. His mind radiated positivity in every direction. He crossed the courtyard and decided to stop by the phone room where he had helped them install their new computer two weeks ago. Father Bob and Saint Thomas Ministries had donated it to them as part of their sponsorship for this temple and all the refugees who came here. It was one of the reasons they were learning English, and why Michael had been hired, as many of them hoped to one day be resettled to other countries. Michael had also been helping them with their papers to be presented to the UN High Commission on Refugees. He poked his head in the small, unpainted room that smelled like old lemons. The abbot of Wat Prok, Pra Sarawon, an elderly monk with gold-rimmed glasses, sat in front of a beige Compaq computer along with a younger monk, whose name Michael didn't know.

"Hi. Everything working ok?"

"Ah, Michael," Pra Sarawon said. "Yes. Yes. Come here. We need your help with something."

Michael pulled a chair next to the abbot. On the computer screen was the website he had been helping them design: www.themonproject.com. "Is the Internet connection working?"

"Yes. My… I never thought I would live to see something like this. This world web is just stupendous. What is this Y2K problem? Is it really going to destroy it?"

"Something about all computers can't recognize the year 2000, a date that ends in '00'. They think it will cause computers worldwide to crash. No one knows. But I'm sure it will work itself out."

"Well, we want to add a photograph to the website."

"Sure." Michael took the mouse and showed them how to drag and drop the file onto the page and how to size the borders.

Pra Sarawon smiled. "Just magic!"

The younger monk spoke. "And can you read this paragraph we are writing? Please check our English is good?"

Michael read it out loud. It told all about their plight: "About their persecution from the current ruling junta of their country, the military dictatorship that oppresses them, routinely slaughters them, and denies them the freedom to practice their own language and culture, a culture that had been in existence for a thousand years, long before there was ever a place called Burma… It's good. Who wrote it?"

"Ramanya and Tissa," Pra Sarawon said.

"My star pupils… So Father Bob kind of explained it to me, but you never use the name Myanmar?"

"No," the young monk said.

"Myanmar is the military's name," Pra Sarawon said. "We, and most people in our country, don't accept it."

"And we had our own country. The Mon were the original

empire in our land," the young monk added.

"I'm sorry, but there are so many dates and names of ancient kings. It's hard to keep track, but I have been trying to learn," Michael said.

Pra Sarawon smiled. "It is fine, Michael. We get confused too. The important thing is what you are doing to help us. We are very grateful."

Father Bob entered the room, surprising all three of them. His black clergy shirt had dark stains of sweat, and he took several deep breaths.

"Bob! What are you doing here?" Michael said.

Bob bowed his head and gave the *wai* greeting. "Pra Sarawon. Michael. Pra Shirra," he said, addressing the young monk last.

"Are you ok?"

"A bit, thanks. Pra Sarawon, I need to speak to you. In private. Do you have time?"

Pra Sarawon rose. "Of course." He crossed to the door.

Bob took a quick glance at Michael. "You finished class for the day?"

"For now."

"Ok. We'll catch up later."

"Sure."

Father Bob and Sarawon left the room. Michael lingered a few moments more, helping the young monk make a couple of changes to the site, then gathered his backpack to leave. He walked across the courtyard toward the red and gold front gates. With each step, the euphoria of his morning class began to fade, and with each step his throat and chest began to tighten just a bit. He pushed open the steel door, and as soon as he left the cocoon of the temple walls, the sensory assault of the gargantuan city slapped him in the face. He stood on the hot, sticky, dirty, noisy corner of the street. He squeezed his hand in and out of a tight fist. Michael's next teaching gig wasn't until five p.m.—a group of secretaries in a school on Silom Road. It was now 10:15 a.m. Six hours and forty-five minutes away. The rest of the day loomed up in front of him like a thick wall, like the thick humid air that choked this city day after day. He heard a police siren scream in the distance.

The cracked sidewalk slithered beneath his feet.

Chapter Four

Alive.

That word swirled around inside Ramanya's head.

Alive, alive, alive… Your family is ALIVE—tumbling over
and over, flipping upside down, sitting upright, moving side to
side—those words would not leave him alone.

Grinding his teeth, his angular jaw jutting out farther than
usual, Ramanya scooped out wet cement on a trowel. He spread it
across a brick and placed that brick on top of a line of others. Almost
everyone from his temple was working on an addition to their east
wing, another dormitory so they could bring in more orphans and
runaway children. As it was near the end of the season of *Khao
Pansa*, they would soon lose the dozen or so laypeople who had
temporarily donned the monk's robes, some for a few days, others

for a few weeks, and come to their temple to perform service works. They wanted to get as much done as possible before those extra bodies went away. Tissa worked beside Ramanya. He was the ox of their group—about one-and-a-half times the size of most the others, with broad shoulders and powerful build. He could produce the results of three men combined.

They had grown up together as children, and almost every memory Ramanya had, Tissa was there: as young kids, sitting in the dusty courtyard of their village, making toys out of sticks and rocks; as young teens, hunting wild boar and guinea fowl in the forest and fishing for eel and mudfish in the creeks; and then the day when they were seventeen that changed both of their lives forever. That was day the men with the black boots came and took their fathers away.

The government soldiers had come in the morning when everyone in the village still lay in their beds. A light rain had been falling when the men broke through the bamboo doors of their huts and pulled Ramanya's father by the hair, dragging him along the ground. His mother had tried to hold onto his legs. Ramanya screamed and picked up a kitchen knife and lunged at one the soldiers but was struck in his face with the butt of a rifle. His father tried to break free, but in the courtyard of the village, a dozen more soldiers had created a circle, firing their weapons in the air to keep the other families inside their homes. Tissa's father was already bound by his hands and feet and lay in a broken clump in the muddy red dirt. The soldiers threw both men in the back of a truck. Ramanya and Tissa ran and ran as long as they could, following the truck until the forest swallowed it whole.

They had heard of things like that happening in other villages, men being dragged away, forced to work as slaves for the military, most never to return again; but that morning was the first time the soldiers had invaded their home. It was the shattering of their childhood, the destruction of innocence. The next week he and Tissa joined the Mon Rebel Army, and the swift stream of violence began, a seven-year torrent of blood that had led directly to the annihilation of his village and the death of his mother and sister sixteen months ago.

****

Ramanya wiped away dried cement from his fingers. Sweat rolled into his eyes. It was all his fault. He should have been there to protect them. He and Tissa had been away on another raid, and it was because of him, because of what he had done, that the military came and burned his village. It was retaliation and revenge, and it had been retaliation and revenge that had driven him to do what he had done beforehand, and it had been retaliation and revenge that had driven the military to do what they had done before that, and before that, and before that; and it was that whole endless cycle of retaliation and revenge, of destruction and death that had been churning on and on for decades, for centuries, that had caused him and Tissa to finally say *enough* and why they had both traveled here together, to this temple.

But now the man in the red shirt says his mother and sister are alive and he had been sent here to find Ramanya and tell him so. While the others were at class this morning, Ramanya had met the man just outside the back wall of the temple.

"Who sent you?" Ramanya had asked.

"Your mother," said the man.

"She's dead. I saw the pile of burnt bodies with my own eyes."

"No, she and your sister left just before it happened. They spent several weeks living in the forest, then made their way to my village, up in the high hills, where the military rarely comes. My family has been taking care of them. They are safe and well hidden. Here, she sent you a note." The man unfolded a piece of tattered paper and handed it to Ramanya.

"She didn't write this. My mother can't write. Or read."

"I wrote it. She told me what to say."

Ramanya looked at the swirling script of his Mon language. It said simply: "We cry for you every day. Know that we love you and wish to touch your face: Tissa."

That last word, the name of his best friend, sent a hot wave through his body. His hand shook as he reached out to hold onto the wall to keep from falling.

"This can't be."

"It is, Pra Ramanya. It is."

"Why has it been so long?"

"It took time for us to save money for this journey."

As soon as the man said *money*, Ramanya's eyes narrowed. The man read his face. "No, sir. I'm not asking you for anything. Just to believe me. Just to come home."

Ramanya stared at the piece of wrinkled paper.

"Sir, the other thing is that your mother is ill. She may not last long. That is the other reason I come to you now."

"What's wrong?"

"It's her lungs. They are getting heavy."

Ramanya could see her, lying in a bed, and he remembered when he was younger she would travel to work at the tannery in the nearby town. He could see her brown-stained fingertips when she would return at night.

"What is your name?"

"Thura."

"Thura, I can't just walk across the border."

"Sir, I know your situation. I know the military will kill you if they find you. But we have a plan. I can get you there. You can trust me."

Ramanya looked at the scar on Thura's chin. He wanted to believe the man. He wanted so much to once again see the face of his mother, hear her voice as he had in the dream last night but hear it while she held him, her arms wrapped around his head as she had done a thousand times when he was a child. His stomach burned at the thought of it, of going home. This temple, these people were his friends and brothers, but it was not home.

"Tell me more…"

****

It was time for a water break, the midmorning heat suffocating, even in the shade of their tin roof. Ramanya put down his trowel, sat down on the edge, and let his feet dangle across the lip of the concrete floor. He could see down into the Chinese cemetery, the wide, sprawling, mostly abandoned plot that backed up against their property. There were a few people jogging along the cracked main driveway that snaked around the tombstones, with many of the stones tilting and leaning over like that building in Italy he had seen pictures of. Deep puddles of water surrounded many of the graves, and sitting on top of some of the tombstones were young Thai boys, holding sticks with strings attached to them and balls of bread tied to the end. They were fishing in the puddles for the small, black freshwater crabs that scurried about. The children would catch them and put them in a pouch so they could be fried later for a delicious snack. Ramanya heard police sirens howling in the distance.

Another siren sliced the air, and then down in the courtyard, a young novice monk began to quickly and loudly blow a whistle.

"Sala! Sala!" he shouted, waving everyone to immediately stop what they were doing and gather in their dining hall.

Ramanya looked over to Tissa. "What's going on?"

"I have no idea," said Tissa as he pulled Ramanya to his feet.

The entire population of their temple made their way to the *sala*. In the courtyard, Ramanya saw Father Bob rushing toward the front gate. He called out his name, and Bob stopped.

"Pra Ramanya. Pra Tissa," Bob said and bowed his head.

"Is everything all right?"

"I'm sorry. I'm in a bit of a hurry. Pra Sarawon will let you

43

know," Bob said. "Is everything all right with the both of you? I'll be in town for the next couple of weeks, then I'll be traveling. Let me know if you need anything."

"Of course," Tissa said. "Thank you again for the computer." Bob nodded then climbed on the back of Tommy's motorbike taxi, and the two of them drove out the front gates.

In the *sala*, Pra Sarawon was waiting to address everyone in the temple. "Good afternoon, brothers. Children. And, of course, our guests," he said, indicating the temporary monks. "There has been some troubling news that I must share with all of you. Father Bob Hanlan from Saint Thomas Ministries, who as you know for the past several years has been so generous in supporting us, has informed me that a short time ago a group of men carrying weapons have taken control of our embassy here in Bangkok."

Gasps and some whistles of approval filled the room. Pra Sarawon held up his hand to stop any more catcalls. "Yes, many of us have strong feelings about the current leaders of our country. Many of us have stories of tears that could fill a river, but I must remind you that violence is not the solution we seek. I must remind you of the story of our great Buddha and the road bandit Angulimala. As you recall, Angulimala was a notorious thief and murderer who wore garlands around his neck, one for each life he had taken. One day he saw the Buddha pass him on a road, and Angulimala picked up his sword and shield intent on slaying him. But no matter how fast he walked, he could not catch up to the Buddha who continued forward at a normal pace. In frustration, Angulimala shouted at the Buddha, 'Stop, monk! Stop!'

"The Buddha turned to him and said, 'I have stopped. It is you, Angulimala, who has not yet stopped.'

"Angulimala was stunned by this and asked the Buddha what he meant. 'What I mean,' began the Buddha, 'is that I have stopped forever doing violence to any living being. But you, you have not. You have no restraint.'

"Angulimala stood in awe of the Buddha and laid down his sword and shield and followed the Buddha to a nearby monastery where he asked and received permission to become a monk. He spent the rest of his years in peace and harmony.

"Now I know that none of us here had anything to do with the events now occurring. It appears to be the work of the Karen"—again gasps and low moans of disapproval—"Yes. I know. But what this will mean is that the authorities here in this country, this country that has been so gracious in allowing us to come and live here, they may be paying closer attention to us for a while. If the police or the military come here or stop you on the street, you must, I repeat, you must extend to them the strongest acts of courtesy and respect. Allow them to do their jobs, as we have nothing to hide."

And then at the very moment Pra Sarawon completed those words, the heavy, pounding sounds of a helicopter grew louder and louder, the temple dogs began to bark and howl, and the walls of the *sala* began to vibrate. The group spilled out into the courtyard where a Thai police chopper hovered about ten meters above them. It filled the sky, nearly motionless, the great gusts of air blowing dust and debris into small cyclones. It remained there for several minutes, until its back tail began to sway from side to side, like a dog deciding whether or not to pounce, and then it rose higher in the air and moved forward and away from them, soon out of sight.

Tissa still gazed up into the sky, shielding his eyes from the sun with his fingers, when Ramanya walked up to him and placed his hand upon his shoulder.

"Pra Tissa. I need to speak with you."

Chapter Five

The neighborhood that Michael lived in, the one that separated his apartment and the temple, was blue collar. Real Thais lived here, very few *farangs*. He was in the trenches, not living in the sanitized, gated, white-people communities. Michael turned right onto his street, Yen Chit Alley. Behind him, from the temple, he heard the pulsing sound of a helicopter rising in the sky. In front of him, auto body shops lined the road, where taxis and *tuk-tuks* were taken for repairs. There were also glass shops and welder bungalows, all feeding off one another. The men toiled in blue shorts and no shirts and with grease and dirt crawling across their skin. Their wives ran the food carts and the small stop-n-shop stores, carved into the alleys about a block apart, that sold everything the slick 7-Eleven stores did but cheaper and without all the fancy labels. Red, white, and blue Thai flags hung from the ceilings in those shops. Shelves and coolers were semi-filled with canned meat, shrimp crackers, candy bars, yogurt, sodas, razor blades, pens, cigarettes, and beer. Cold Beer. Just-above-freezing beer. Half-liter bottles. Forty baht apiece, about a buck twenty.

Sweat covered Michael's back and neck as he stopped outside JK Foods, two blocks from his high-rise building. He liked this store the best and often came here because the middle-aged woman who ran it always gave him a free red-bean cake whenever he bought something. Her name was Nona, and she had a megawatt smile that compensated for her thick belly. Her husband owned the tire store two rows down. Nona pressed her hands together and greeted Michael.

"Sa-wat-dii, khâ, Michael. Sabaai-dii mái?"

"Fine, yes, thank you, Nona."

"And how are the monks?" Everyone on this street knew where he went each morning.

"They send you their blessings," said Michael.

"Cigarettes?" asked Nona.

"Yes. Krung-Thep. One pack."

"Anything else?"

"Two bottles of water. A can of Fanta Lemon. Two Bic razors. A lighter—that orange one there is fine."

Nona glided around the dark hole in the alley that was her store, gathering his order. She pulled two red plastic bags from a box and carefully packed each item as if they were bird's eggs.

"And some beer? Do you want some beer as usual?"

Michael stared at the horizontal cooler that inched onto the oil-stained sidewalk. *No,* he told himself. *No.*

"Yes. Give me four half liters of Singha." He couldn't look her in the eye when he spoke. He was certain that behind her smile, she knew what he was really all about.

Didn't everyone know? Everyone on this street who smiled and waved at him? He was the only white person who lived there so he stuck out like snow in July, and everyone knew he taught those troublesome monks at the Burmese temple, and everyone knew he carried around those plastic bags, heavy with bottles, morning, noon, and night.

He walked the gauntlet of all the eyes watching him and the voices whispering about him. Sweat now covered his green, button-up Oxford shirt. One last stop. Food. He needed food. As usual, Michael had not eaten since the night before when he passed out—whenever that was. Diagonally across from his high-rise sat a trifecta of food carts. One sold spicy pork. One sold pad Thai noodles. The other sold roast chicken breasts with spicy orange sauce. Michael shelled out one hundred baht for three chicken breasts. They knew him too.

Sa-wat-dii, khâ, Michael! *Sabaai-dii mái,* Michael! How are you? We love you. You are so handsome. Will you meet my daughter? Ha ha! So funny! You have the best food. I'm sure your daughter is lovely. I apologize. I'm very busy today. Just give me the food, and may peace be with your family.

Michael crossed the street and entered the small lobby of his building. Louis Mansion was a generic ten-story apartment building that sat on the corner of Yen Chit Alley and Thanon Chan. There was Sherri, a flat-faced but buxom Thai girl who worked as a receptionist in the building her mother Rose had owned for twenty years. Sherri always walked out of her glass cage when Michael came home.

"Good morning. And the monks were good?" She had wild, dark hair, thick like a raven-colored medusa, and always put her hand on Michael's back as she escorted him to the elevators. She had a squashed nose but always smelled great—like a honeysuckle bush.

"Sherri. You look lovely today."

"I do it only for you. Mmm... nice strong back. So when you let me come clean your room?"

The plastic bags tugged at Michael's fingers, and his quiet air-cooled room screamed for him. "Thanks. You are so sweet. But I can clean my own room."

"When you give me English lesson? Private?"

"Sherri… You know I am very busy."

"My mother wants cook for us."

"Absolutely. Maybe next week? So sorry. Love your new shoes. Have to go. Have so much work to do."

"Mmm. Yes. With all those butterflies you bring home each night. I can be a butterfly too, you know. And you don't even have to pay me."

Yeah, they *all* knew what he was really about. Sweat kept pouring from his neck. Michael scurried toward the single, copper-colored lift. "Sherri, my darling… Have a nice day."

The elevator doors creaked shut, like an old man clearing his throat full of phlegm.

****

Once inside his room, Michael tore off his wet shirt, kicked away his shoes, cranked the air conditioner down to fifteen degrees Celsius, and flipped off the cap on his first bottle of beer. He stared at it. The carbonation in the bottle sizzled and popped, and the cold glass numbed his fingers. The chilled beer covered his tongue as it slid down his throat and landed with a frozen thud in his stomach. He took another tug. And then another… The downward slide was on, just like he had done most every day for the past three months.

Michael lit a cigarette, the pungent local Thai ones that tasted like sucking on a sweat sock. But they were cheap, and they had a hell of a kick. The beer flowed again and again. His empty stomach, having had no food since yesterday, sucked in the alcohol like a dry sponge and sent a mainline shot of a buzz directly to his brain. He would eat, but not yet. The high was faster, stronger, more intense on an empty stomach, and now that he had once again taken a trip down this razor-sharp route, it was exactly what he wanted: the strongest, fastest, most intense cheap-beer high that he could possibly get.

His world shrank. There was no big city on this side of the sliding glass doors. No people wanting to talk to him, no one watching him, no one expecting anything from him. There was nothing. Only himself and his bottles and this quiet room. It was a small studio apartment. A half-size refrigerator sat along the main wall. Next to that, sitting on a wooden chair, was an old TV that got three channels: CNN, MTV, and a local Thai sports channel that showed kickboxing matches nonstop. Two sliding glass doors led to a small balcony. A king-size bed took up most of the space with the weird pink flowered sheets that had come with it, which Michael kept saying he was going to replace but never did. An armoire, in which he kept his four dress shirts, three ties, and three pairs of dress pants, stood tilting on only three good legs. In the bathroom, a small spigot stuck out of the wall where only cold water fell for his showers. A toilet with a built-in bidet completed his "luxury" suite.

This was his home. This was where he had ended up, just past age thirty, and now, after his morning purchase, with about $130 to his name.

The first bottle downed in less than ten minutes, Michael cracked open his second and then settled into the chair next to his desk. A quick look at yesterday's *International Herald Tribune*: Chechnya blah, blah, blah. Y2K blah, blah, blah. Neanderthals Probably Ate People—at last, something interesting. His baseball team, the Atlanta Braves, were heading to the playoffs again. They'd probably choke like they usually did.

Bottle number three. The exhilarating high collapsed under the weight of its own stupidity. His body now felt like it weighed five hundred pounds. He took off the remainder of his clothes and wrapped himself only in his towel. He slumped to the floor at the foot of his bed. Turned on the TV, then turned it off. CNN sucked. Bangkok sucked. The monks sucked. He sucked. He lit one cigarette off the end of the other and tossed the burnt butts onto the floor. Maybe he'd start a fire. Maybe he'd burn himself to death. That might be the best way out.

His brain was shutting down, on the verge of passing out. Time to eat. His stomach was lashing out for something solid. But not just yet. Suck in more cigarettes, pound down more booze. More, more, more. Push it as far as he could go. It was nothing less than self-flagellation. Like the Reverend Dimmesdale in *The Scarlet Letter* that he and every other high school student in America had to read. Those passages of the Reverend whipping himself to atone for his sins, for his lustful thoughts and actions, had always stuck out to him, and that was what he was now doing. Atoning for his sins. Whipping himself, slashing his skin. *But wait a minute—what sins?* Yes, he'd done one or two stupid things in his life—well, one *very* stupid thing—but why was he really doing this to himself? He didn't know. He wasn't that bad. He wasn't a horrible person. Was he?

He didn't know. He looked across the street through the sliding glass doors. There was the palm tree he liked to look at. It rose from an alley between two cinder-block stores and was thick and full and brilliant green and was so different from the faces of the surrounding buildings stained in black and brown from years of pollution. That tree was always shining out, covered in different types of light. In the mornings, it was often bathed in a pink or orange glow. In the evenings, a nice golden yellow. At night, the streetlights and neon signs of busy Thanon Chan lit it up in a brilliant white. It almost seemed to smile at him, waving at him to come over to it, and he kept saying one day he would actually walk over there and stand beside it and place his hand on its trunk, but at the same time it was so perfect the way it was, he didn't want to ruin it.

Yes, he really, really liked that tree.

He crawled over to the fridge and took out the three roast chicken breasts and the three small plastic cups of spicy sweet orange sauce. His towel fell off his waist, and Michael continued on, sitting naked on the cold tile floor at the foot of his bed and tore into the chicken like a wolverine. The smoky flavors of the fire, the basil and lemongrass and chili peppers burned on his lips, and then he dipped it all in the orange paste. Orgasmic. He had denied himself food until he could no longer stand it, and then when he finally ate, it was a double-barreled shotgun of flavor and satisfaction jammed down his throat.

He slammed down his final beer, and at 12:40 p.m., Michael Shaw finally fell asleep.

Chapter Six

The headquarters for Saint Thomas Ministries Worldwide, Thailand Mission were located in the rear of an old, nearly forgotten strip mall, overlooking the Chao Phraya River. Father Bob rushed into the wide-open office space that covered the entire second floor. His desk sat in the middle of seven other empty desks, and he collapsed in his chair and stared out the window. The waves of the river winked and shimmered in the sun. He opened his bottom drawer, took out a jar of peanut butter and a plastic spoon, and jammed some in his mouth.

Father Timothy came out of his private office, put on his black clergy jacket, and locked the door. He was thin, close to Bob's height, in his early sixties with short-cropped gray hair. "So... What have you done now?"

Bob continued to look out the window. "What makes you

think I did anything?"

"I heard sirens outside so that usually means you are involved."

"Haven't you left yet? I came here expecting to have the office to myself."

"Aran is on the way to pick me up. The others left for Chiang Mai an hour ago… It will be a nice retreat. The air up there is cool this time of year. You sure you won't come?"

Bob turned his chair around to face Timothy. "Am I now invited? I thought we had agreed my absence would be most welcome."

"We are in the business of forgiving."

"I'll stay here. Cheers."

Father Timothy dropped his chin to his chest for a moment, then took a step toward Bob. "We need to finish this. What happened last month in Yangon—"

"Rangoon. For me, it will always be called Rangoon."

"Do I need to remind you how fortunate it was we were able to bail you out? Otherwise, you'd still be sitting in that squalid prison. You can't go off half-cocked like that. You jeopardize not only our mission here in this country but the safety of everyone who works for us. If you do something like that again, I'm sorry, but you'll be on your own."

"I've got it. Yes. Things got out of control. Haven't we already gone over this?"

"You seem to have a hearing problem, and I have a sense you are up to something. I mean, really. Secret meetings with student rebels? Starting a riot? Getting arrested? At the same moment I'm inside with members of the Myanmar—don't say Burma—government, assuring them we are there for humanitarian reasons only and we are not there to cause trouble? We *all* could have been arrested."

Bob sat silently and rubbed his fingers together. Aran, a portly Thai man who worked as their lead driver, entered from a side door and took a set of keys off a hook on the wall.

"Hello, Father Bob. You coming with us?"

Bob and Timothy locked eyes. "No," Bob said. "How's your daughter, Aran?"

"Top of her class. Thanks for the tuition."

"No worries. Glad I could help."

Father Timothy picked up a duffel bag that sat by the door. "Stay safe," he said to Bob. "We'll talk more when I get back next week."

Aran and Timothy walked out the front door, leaving Bob

alone in the office.

Bob stared at the ceiling. Timothy obviously hadn't heard yet about the shitstorm now happening at the embassy. But once he did, the judgment would be swift, and he would join most everyone else in saying Bob had a hand in it. Directly or indirectly. It didn't matter. It didn't matter that Bob had had no idea machine guns would be whipped out and the embassy here in Bangkok taken over. He had thought it would be a "simple" street protest—if there ever is such a thing.

He had received a message two weeks ago at his home. Bob responded to a knock on his door to find a small Thai girl of about nine or ten with a tray of garlands, flowers sold for people to give as offerings at the many street shrines around the city; but his house was far away from any shrine. The girl smiled and pushed out the tray and motioned with her eyes for Bob to pick up the top string of flowers. The soft light-blue and yellow petals tumbled in his fingers, and he felt a folded piece of paper taped to the bottom. Bob gave her a one hundred baht note, and she went on her way without ever saying a word. Once in his house, Bob unfolded the grid-ruled paper, from a child's school notebook, and on it was one handwritten word: Fortnight.

He knew it had been from Jonny, a Burmese rebel leader, the

man with the pompadour he had seen on the embassy roof this morning and whom Bob had met on his trip to Rangoon last month. The trip Timothy was so hacked off about, and with good reason. It had been a precariously arranged visit to meet with members of the Myanmar Ministry of Religious Affairs. They had wanted to discuss the possibility of Saint Thomas opening a boarding house in the slums of the Burmese capital city, to help with health outreach programs aimed at the Rangoon street kids. Father Timothy had been very careful to explain that it would be a humanitarian project only and not an excuse for proselytizing. It was supposed to have been a series of peaceful, respectful, fact-finding meetings, and they had hoped and prayed to lay the groundwork for these and other future projects during that trip.

Then Bob blew the whole thing apart.

****

St. Mary's Church, a gorgeous red-brick and stone, intricate, multi-spired cathedral, stood in downtown Rangoon as a reminder of the country's colonial past. As some of the population in Burma had remained Catholic over the years, it was active with daily services though tightly controlled and regularly watched by the military. Still, it had been fairly easy for Bob to slip out unnoticed on the first night of their visit. Timothy had retired early, and before they left Bangkok, Bob had sent a message to a rebel leader he had met a few weeks before. They had arranged to meet that evening and plan an event for the next day.

The night air was quiet, too quiet for a city its size, as Bob walked down the back staircase and then to one of the guardhouses. He knew the Burmese sentry by name and in the past had brought him gifts from Thailand. Bob bribed him with a carton of Marlboro Reds. The sentry let Bob out the gate without incident. Two blocks away was an auto parts shop where members of the Vigorous Burmese Student Warriors—and, yes, that name should have been a red flag—were meeting in the warehouse.

The young man Bob had met once in Bangkok greeted him at the side door and ushered him inside. About two dozen men gathered in a room that smelled like wet cardboard and motor oil. Bob was introduced to their leader, Jonny, and his eyes immediately gravitated toward his unusual hair.

"So you're a fan of Elvis?" Bob asked.

"Of course," Jonny said. "He is the king."

One of the young men leaned forward to Bob and pointed at Jonny. "He's a soldier."

"In a rebel army?"

61

"No. With the government!"

"Pardon?" Bob said.

"I'm a reserve soldier now," Jonny said. "But, yes, I was with them for several years."

To Bob, that explained why, despite his flamboyant hairstyle, Jonny gave off a sense of toughness, even a touch of ruthlessness.

"I know how they think," Jonny said and tapped his finger against his head. "Not everyone in the army supports the way things are done here. They just don't know what to do. That is why we must show the people will support them if they try to change."

"Let me know what you want me to do," said Bob.

"Are you sure you want to get involved in something like this? Won't your superiors disagree?" asked Jonny.

Bob hesitated a moment, then answered the question. "They have their way of doing things. And I've been following along, but I agree, something else needs to be done. Something different. Something visual, not behind the scenes."

They decided to hold a street protest the next morning at 10:00 a.m., just outside the front gates of St. Mary's Church, along Bo Aung Kyaw Street, and across from the offices of the *Myanmar Times*. Bob originally had thought it would be a brilliant spot for a protest. Instant media coverage. All the newspaper had to do was look out their windows. But in retrospect…

It began with the usual speeches, decrying the lack of democracy in their country, but then Jonny took over, a small man but with a booming voice. He began a series of shouts and chants that quickly pulled in swarms of people from the surrounding streets. Bob had been right in the middle of it, shouting and pumping his fist and handing out flyers and getting pushed around as the crowds grew bigger, and as the windows of the *Myanmar Times* did in fact fling open. Then the sirens came, the trucks of soldiers came, nightsticks in their hands. Blood began to pour, and the chaos of a full-fledged riot exploded outside the gates of St. Mary's Church at the very moment that inside the cathedral, Father Timothy was sitting down to tea with members of the Myanmar Ministry of Home Affairs and the Ministry of Religious Affairs, explaining to them that they were not coming there to cause any trouble.

A riot cop punched Bob in the stomach several times and then bound his hands and threw him into the back of a police truck. He was taken to a nearby station and put into a squalid holding cell with only a small hole in the center of the concrete floor for people to relieve themselves. Several of the other protesters were tossed in there as well, many of them bruised and bleeding with no attempts from the Burmese police to offer any help. Bob did what he could to clean some of the wounds, removing shards of glass or splinters of wood left from the riot cops' batons. It was the second time in his life he had ever been imprisoned, and while there was an odd sense of familiarity, a sense of resignation to it, the overwhelming feeling was one of dread.

After two hours, two guards came into the cell and took Bob out. Bob demanded that he be allowed to contact the British embassy, telling them he had diplomatic credentials and he should be afforded proper treatment. They ignored him. He was led to a solitary room where a man with cut and bruised knuckles was waiting for him. They used metal shackles to bind Bob's hands and feet to the chair. The two guards left the room. The man had a lazy eye that glanced sideways at the wall as he circled around Bob several times, his mouth open and his whitish tongue hanging out, almost leering at Bob. Bob tensed his body, anticipating the thundering blows ready to pound his face… But then the door opened and a police captain walked in, waved his hand across his neck, and told Mr. Knuckles to untie him. As the two guards led him out the room, the captain stopped Bob and pushed him against the wall. The captain dug his finger hard into the skin just below Bob's chin. Bob knew enough Burmese to understand what he said: "This is not the end. It is just the beginning."

The guards led him out the front doors and back onto the street. There, a private driver was waiting for him with a small blue van. The driver handed Bob a note, and Bob recognized the handwriting as Father Timothy's. It said simply: Stupid move. The van went on and quickly left the city, heading back toward the Thai border, carrying Bob and only Bob, no Father Timothy, no one else. Eventually they arrived at the checkpoint in Hpayarthonesu across from Three Pagodas Pass on the Thai side. Bob was dropped off at the red and white gates. Two Burmese soldiers grabbed him by each arm and marched him right up to the border, then pushed him forward to stumble back into Thailand alone.

Alone.

Bob squirmed at his desk. Timothy was wrong in saying they were lucky to get him out. The junta had done that just to save face, but they would not forget. He was certain they were behind the shadows that Bob now saw following him most everywhere he went; those shadows were either Myanmar Intelligence or more likely local goons hired by them to keep tabs on his movements. They would bide their time and pounce when ready, and today's events now gave them the perfect excuse.

He grunted and shook his head. He turned on the TV and scanned the channels, stopping at CNN and BBC Worldwide.

Nothing. He turned on the radio and set the dial for Virgin Station 1. Commercial, commercial, commercial. Newscaster comes on. More about Y2K. More about the WTO. Then: "And in breaking news, in Bangkok, Thailand, it appears armed rebels have stormed the embassy of Myanmar and taken all personnel hostage. Thai military units have arrived and stationed themselves outside the embassy. There have been unsuccessful attempts to contact the rebels, and at this time, no list of demands or reasons for the attack have been made public. In Japan..."

Bob turned it off. Not much he could do with that. But the word *hostage*, as soon as it penetrated his ear, made his heart pound. His breaths came quicker and more shallow, and his chest and throat felt like they were filling up with cement. He dug the spoon into the peanut butter jar, swirled it around, and pulled out a massive mound. He crammed the large spoonful in his mouth and let his lips and tongue surround it, pressing down and sucking on the smooth texture as hard they possibly could.

Chapter Seven

Ramanya and Tissa leaned against the outside back wall of the *sala*, out of view from the others. Tissa smoked a cigarette. Even though their abbot allowed them to do so, Tissa always felt a bit guilty and preferred to do it with no one watching. He had offered one to Ramanya, but Ramanya refused.

Ramanya had just finished telling Tissa about the man in the red shirt, the white cat, and the dream. The two of them stood in silence. They could hear squeals of the children playing in the courtyard.

Tissa looked at the crumpled note, then handed it back to Ramanya. "I don't think you should go."

"You don't?"

"No. How do you know this isn't a trap? A way for the

military to lure you back there? They may be waiting for you."

"They will always be waiting for me," said Ramanya. "They will never forget."

"What makes you think this man is telling the truth?" asked Tissa.

"He knew things about them. He described their clothes. He described the scar on my sister's arm."

"They could have gotten all that from photos they stole from your home before they burned it down."

Ramanya nodded. "Yes, but he also knew the code word my mother and I had created in case I was in hiding and needed to reach her."

Tissa raised his eyebrows. "Really? What was that?"

"You," said Ramanya, pointing at the note. "Your name— Tissa."

Tissa smiled and shook his head. He took one last drag of the cigarette, stubbed it out in the dirt, and cupped the butt in his palm. He would throw it in the rubbish bin later.

"He could have guessed that too. Everyone knows we've always been side by side in whatever we have done."

"That is why I speak to you now. You are my oldest and most important friend. You are the one person whose trust and opinion I value over all others."

"That's quite a burden you're placing on me, my friend," said Tissa.

"Brother, I don't mean to burden you—"

"I know," interrupted Tissa.

Ramanya sighed. "We left too soon."

Ramanya retraced in his mind the days after the burning of their village. He and Tissa had taken to the forest, living in a cave for nearly two weeks, living on grub worms, papaya, and the occasional roasted rat. If what the man said was true, they had probably not been far from where his mother and sister had fled. It was that word Michael had taught him: tragic.

For the first few days, he and Tissa had not said a word to each other, and then one morning Tissa rolled over on the ground beside the white ash heap of their dead morning fire. "I'm done, " he said.

"What do you mean?" asked Ramanya.

Tissa stood up, his head nearly touching the slick wet top of the cave. "What I mean is that I don't want this anymore. We accomplish nothing. All we do is kill and bring death to those we love. I'm leaving. I want you to come with me. There is nothing for us here anymore. There is nothing to fight for."

"And go where?"

"Across the border. To Bangkok. To the Mon temple there. From there we can try to move to other countries. Australia. America. Our families our dead. If we stay here, we are dead. All the fighting we have done. Has it changed anything at all?"

Ramanya used his finger to stir the wet sand on the floor of the cave. "No. You are right…It is time to go."

Bit by bit they ventured into nearby towns and sold their weapons to back-alley profiteers until they had enough to pay the smuggling fees. They made plans to cross into Thailand, wading through the river at Mae Sot, avoiding the military posts. Once in the country, they walked and hitchhiked to Bangkok and arrived at the temple sixteen months ago. After sleeping for nearly three days, they shaved their heads, put on the robes, and vowed to leave their world in Burma, their world of violence, far, far behind.

Ramanya looked at Tissa, waiting for his response.

"So what do you think?"

"I don't know," said Tissa. "Why don't we contact Father Bob and discuss it with him? He knows people on this side of the border that may be able to help. He often travels to Three Pagodas

Pass."

"Yes, I thought of that," said Ramanya.

"Why don't we... What was the phrase Michael taught us? Ah—*sleep on it.*"

"Yes...but you know if this situation at the embassy continues, it won't take much time before the military comes to close the entire border. Then it will be impossible to cross. This man said he will wait here in the city only until tomorrow for my answer."

"Yes, but you and I also know how the military over there moves. It will be a couple of days before anything happens. Two, maybe three. They will be preoccupied with what's going on now. You have a little bit of time."

"A little," responded Ramanya. "But not much."

Tissa shook his head. "The Karen," he said. "Always causing trouble."

"Yes, they are difficult. But us Mon are not blameless. We have blood on our hands as well."

"No, I know," said Tissa. "But I had hoped you and I had escaped all that when we came here. I had hoped we had left it all behind... in the ashes of our home fires."

Ramanya wiped sweat from his brow. "One's past is never far away."

Tissa placed his arm on Ramanya's shoulder and gave him a tight squeeze of support. They walked back around the building and into the courtyard where they saw the reason the group of kids been squealing with delight: one boy had a ball of string that the white cat was busy chasing, leaping in the air and running in and out of the children's legs.

They went to the *sala* and joined the others for their noon meal, the last meal they would eat for the day. Afterward, Tissa and Ramanya climbed back up to the work site and resumed scooping out cement and laying down bricks. For the next couple of hours, Ramanya fell into the physical rhythm of building the wall, but inside he felt knotted up, painful and sore, the muscles in his chest stretched tight like vines pulled too far. He tried to visualize the possible reunion, the moment when he might see his mother and sister, risen from the dead. He tried to feel the embrace, the moment his skin pressed against theirs, the warm rush, the puff of air as his mother whispered in his ear. But then he saw the government soldiers of Myanmar, the soldiers he had spent years fighting, their rifles pointed at his head, and he heard the click of the trigger, saw the puff of smoke from the barrel, and felt the bullets slice his skull into shreds.

Later, the temple bell rang out. All put down their tools and gathered in the *viharn* for their afternoon devotions. Ramanya tried to empty his mind as much as possible to allow the guidance and wisdom he needed to arrive unimpeded; but again, as in the morning, he had no luck. Images continued to fill his mind: the man in the red shirt, the smile of his sister, and the pile of dead bodies sitting in the middle of his village, burnt and still smoldering, embers glowing white and red like the eyes of wolves staring out at night from a forest.

Chapter Eight

At 4:15 p.m., Michael's alarm clock buzzed to life. He rolled over in his bed and swatted it dead. It took a moment for him to realize what he was supposed to do, then he remembered he had to teach at 5:00, and then he also remembered the stupidity of what he had done all morning. Again.

He slowly lifted himself onto the cold tile floor, his body bloated and feeling heavy. His mouth and throat were excruciatingly dry, and he opened up his mini fridge to crack open a bottle of water. It gushed down his esophagus and into his stomach, and it felt majestic. Next, he stumbled into his bathroom and turned on the spigot in the wall. Only cold water came out. It was a shock at first but soon helped him to shake off the cobwebs of his morning routine. He dried off, and since he had recently buzzed his hair down almost like the monks, he didn't have to worry about that. He looked in the mirror: his face was puffy, and his eyes were red, so he reached for his Visine drops, but the bottle was empty. There was a Boots Pharmacy near the office building where he taught, so he would have to stop in there to get some, as a well as a bottle of that electrolyte drink that tasted like thick, super sweet Gatorade.

He put on a white cotton Oxford shirt then a pair of brown dress pants, but he had trouble connecting the waist. He was disgusted. He was getting fat. He had just bought those pants two months ago, and they had been too big. Now they were too tight. That was it. He was coming home tonight, drinking lots of water. He would go down to the soup cart on the corner and get a big bowl of spicy fish ball soup with lots of bok choy and carrots, and then he would come home, read a book, get some deep, sober sleep, then get up in the morning and go for a run in the Chinese cemetery before it got too hot.

He grabbed his book bag and took the elevator to the lobby. Sherri was there as always.

"Going out?" she said. "Say hello to the butterflies for me."

Michael just smiled and kept walking, out the front door and into that thick wall of heat known as everyday weather in Bangkok. He hailed a *songthaew*, a pickup truck taxi, and climbed in the back, sitting on a bench with half a dozen Thais who just smiled at him. Sweat began to soak through his shirt.

It was a quick trip up to Silom Road, and the truck let him out a block away from his building. Silom was always buzzing, and one could see all of Bangkok on this one street. There were the slick stores, high-rise office buildings and hotels, American chain restaurants like Sizzler and Fridays; and there were also the endless food carts with their cheap plastic chairs and tables, and the small ramshackle alleys overflowing with fresh fruit, produce, and spices. And then there was Patpong Road with all its go-go bars. It stood directly across from the office building Michael now entered, and the blast of near-arctic air inside felt amazing and helped to wake him up some more. On the sixth floor was a school for secretaries where he taught for ninety minutes, three evenings a week. Before he went in, he ducked into the men's room and peeled off some paper towels to blot away as much of the sweat from under his arms and around his neck as possible. His hands shook a bit, and he grabbed them to steady them. He took one last look in the mirror. "Let's do it," he said.

He walked confidently down the hall and through the glass doors of the school. Endless smiles and greetings and bowing of heads were waiting for him. The switch was on. He was no longer that idiot who had cowered drunkenly on the floor all morning. He was Michael Shaw: Super-Teacher. A group of twelve young Thai women were waiting for him in the conference room, and he walked in like a rock star.

For the next ninety minutes, Michael thought he was nothing short of amazing. He had the girls work in groups, practice answering phones, practice dealing with customer complaints, practice pronunciation, practice writing emails. He was loose. He was funny. Those lovely Thai girls giggled at his every joke, and at the end of class, a group of four of them came up to Michael.

The girl known as Fawn spoke first. "Michael, we are going out to dinner tonight. There is a nice restaurant at Silom Mall. Can you come with us?"

Tina and Jackie chimed in. "Yes, Michael, can you please come with us? Maybe after we go disco bowling."

They are gorgeous, thought Michael. They were so clean. Blouses and skirts perfectly pressed. Clean hair perfectly cut. They wore just the right amount of makeup. They were young and smooth and so inviting.

"Wow, thank you so much. But I already have plans tonight. I'd really like to. Maybe next week?"

They pouted in disappointment, which made them even

sexier, but Michael said goodbye, and as he walked out the door, the principal of the school, a middle-aged Thai woman known as Miss Song, handed Michael an envelope. He had forgotten it was payday.

"Thanks you so much," Miss Song said. "You are doing such great job. The girls are learning so much."

"It's my pleasure, Miss Song. I'll see you next week," Michael said and pressed his hands together and bowed his head.

Back out on Silom Road, the sun had nearly set, and Michael looked in the envelope where there was ten thousand Thai baht in cash, which was about $300. That was for nine hours work. Not bad, but he needed more gigs like this. Father Bob had been generous in setting him up with that free apartment, but as much as liked working for the monks, it did not pay, so the only spending money he had came from jobs like this.

That apartment. Suddenly it seemed like a tomb. Why had he blown off those girls? He did nothing anymore except sit in that apartment guzzling beer until he passed out. Getting fat. Hiding. His whole world had been collapsing upon itself for months, like a dying star, its rotten core crumbling under the density of its own dead mass, until nothing was left but a black hole, where no light or matter could escape.

Still, he needed to just go back there. He needed to take a

break tonight. Get sleep. *Get up tomorrow and go for a run and sweat it all out,* he thought as he crossed the street and headed for Patpong Road.

****

His first stop was the Pub Madrid, a small dive bar halfway down the alley, and as soon as he walked in, someone called out his name. *Christ, I'm a regular here now. At this dump? How pathetic.* It was that guy from New Zealand, Jim or Joe or something like that, and he motioned for Michael to sit down next to him.

"Whatcha drinking, mate? I'll buy the first one for you," said Jim/Joe.

"I'll have a beer Chang. Just one tonight."

"Just one! In a couple of months the world is gonna end! Didn't you know that? Live it up!" he said and slapped Michael on the back. He motioned for the bartender, a woman named Mamma Noi. "Hey, Mamma, can you play that song?"

Mama Noi put a cassette tape in the stereo, and the opening drum roll to REM's "It's the End of the World as We Know It (And I Feel Fine)" came on, and everyone tried to sing along with the fast parts, but everyone knew the chorus.

Baseball played on the TV. Final weekend of the regular

season, Pirates against the Mets, via the magic of those blinking tin cans circling high above the earth. The playoffs would soon start. October in the States, along the East Coast most importantly, was Michael's favorite time of year. The thirteen months he had lived in Los Angeles, that had been one of the biggest things Michael missed: seasons. Not the same boring weather every day, every month, but four distinct times of year, each with their charms, but fall, well, fall was simply the best. Chilly mornings, warm afternoons, the first wafts of burning pinewood drifting out of chimneys, leaves beginning to turn. Football, back to school, state fairs, giant corndogs, and bumper cars. This time last year, he would have been sitting in one of his favorite watering holes back home in Columbia, South Carolina, probably either The Art Bar or Yesterday's Tavern, watching another game. This time last year, he would have still been married—though not happily; he would have had money in the bank—though mostly borrowed. This time last year, he'd never yet had to scrounge to get work as a dishwasher just to keep from starving, or sleep under bridges with packs of feral cats picking at his head. This time last year, he could never, ever have imagined where he would be sitting, right now, at this time this year.

He looked around at all the white men, the *farangs*, sitting their fat asses on the barstools, their arms around some Thai hostess, and Michael knew he was right in the process of ending up just like them. A fucking cliché. The bloated, drunk expatriate with the young sex toy on his payroll. He had entered the Disgusting-Western-Man-Hiding-Out-in-Southeast-Asia Factory, and the assembly line was dragging him along, ready to spit him out onto the waste heap of the thousands of others who had rusted and corroded into oblivion. *So put a stop to it. Finish this beer and get the fuck out of here. Go back to the apartment and stare at the walls. It's better than this. In fact, just go HOME. Go see the leaves changing into red and gold. Go pile some wood in a fireplace. Go sit in your empty house all alone and stare at* those *walls and wait for your world to finish collapsing on yourself...*

"Fuck it," Michael said. He motioned to Mamma Noi. "Give me another beer and a shot."

Jim/Joe slapped him on the back. "There ya go! Now that's the spirit. Next one's on me!"

More shots and beers and slaps and shouts and sing-alongs and then the fear of ending up like the rest of these sorry lost souls faded away; Michael wouldn't make it that far. He was pulling a *Leaving Las Bangkok*, a slow suicide, so at least he would spare himself the indignity.

Michael wandered outside back onto Patpong Road with all

the neon signs of all the go-go bars, the strip clubs, the crush of people and all the touts standing outside all the bars shouting that they had the best girls, they had the best drinks, but they were all the same, and Michael stumbled into a place called The Thigh Bar with the glitter mirrors and more *farangs* with their arms around more girls, and with girls dancing on the stage to '80s heavy metal songs. He went into the bathroom to pee, and then as he was finishing, a young Thai woman with a tight, two-piece red jumpsuit and heavy makeup appeared next to him.

"I want to eat your cock," she said.

And there you had it, why the hell not, he nearly fell walking out the bathroom as she led him upstairs to rows of small dark cubicles with black lights and padded benches that smelled like stale beer and urine and then her hands and then her mouth and then his hands and then lying down and then rolling and thrusting and no protection mister bareback rider, but who the fuck cares, not the first time, and then it was done, and then he paid, and then he was back out on the street again.

Michael stumbled out the back end of the street, clutching his head tightly between both his hands, just like that famous painting *The Scream*, and he wandered over to King Rama IV road, under the statue of that famous leader, heading down the cobblestone sidewalk jammed with food carts, across from Lumphini Park, its wide green fields lit up at night in a brilliant white light, and all the noises and lights and smells and voices and everything swirled violently around him, spinning him around in a kaleidoscopic rage, and then it finally happened. It was like a battering ram striking his gut. His face trembled, his knees buckled, and he collapsed to the ground. He started sobbing uncontrollably, howling, screaming, everything pouring out of him, all these months, all these years, all the stupidity and disappointment and bad decisions he had ever made, as people stepped over him and around him, ignoring him. Soon he was hovering above himself, looking down on his broken, crumpled ball of flesh, curled like a baby on the sidewalk, and as he rose higher in the sky, the sounds of his crying and wailing mixed with police sirens and helicopters. He rose up, up, up, and up until his body was nothing, nothing but a tiny speck of dust, barely visible, clinging tenuously on a vast empty plain, and then at last, he simply just disappeared.

Chapter Nine

It was nighttime now as Father Bob Hanlan still sat at his desk, his reading lamp being the only light in the dark office. He had been hiding out all day. Every hour or so he had scanned the radio and TV for more news about the embassy, but not much had been released to the public. So far, at least, it appeared no one had been killed.

One of his main duties was coordinating all the volunteers Saint Thomas had working in the field, so he had been going over their schedules and planning when he would go out and visit each one. It helped take his mind off what was happening at the embassy.

There was the American lad Michael working here at the Mon temple, so he was easy to see. There was the Scottish couple Chrissie and James who ran community health programs at their camp near Kanchanaburi. There was the Australian girl Noelle who taught at a school in Pattaya. The British girl Martha who worked with farmers near Chiang Mai. And there was the other Brit Ian who was designing water sanitation projects near the border with Laos. They each came for six to twelve months at a time, volunteering their time for free room and board and not much else.

Bob stood up. It was time to go home. He turned off his desk lamp. The neon glow from all the shops on Charoen Krung Road poured through the window and filled the room. Father Timothy's office was next to the front and Bob paused there a moment, recalling the conversation they had had earlier that day. Timothy had been right, of course, but because of the recent tension between them, Bob had never brought it to Timothy's attention that in the past few weeks he felt like he was being watched, being followed. Timothy wouldn't have wanted to hear it anyway and would have told Bob he was just being paranoid. Maybe… But now with what was going on at the embassy, well, that was something else, wasn't it? That pushed things to a different level indeed.

Bob locked the office door, walked down the stone staircase to the ground floor, and hailed a taxi.

The taxi turned off the main road onto Alley 79, a narrow and dark path that cut through rows of short houses standing behind concrete fences. The driver moved slowly at first, as there was not much room to navigate around the occasional groups of people walking along the road. They passed a small pack of women, housewives by the way they dressed in plain skirts and aprons and balanced plastic tubs of vegetables on their heads. They passed a group of men, probably their husbands, sitting on a blanket, drinking from bottles of Johnnie Walker Whisky and smoking cigarettes. They turned down another alley and came to a small clearing where someone had set up a makeshift outdoor theater with a video projector and a bed sheet. Jackie Chan leapt across the sheet as a few dozen people sat on the ground in front of him.

Bob heard the sounds of a motorcycle coming up behind them. The engine revved up and down a few times. The taxi turned again down another narrow alley. The motorcycle came close to the rear bumper of the car a couple of times, then drifted back. The driver adjusted the radio. An oldies station. "Just the Way You Look Tonight" by Frank Sinatra came on. Bob looked out the back window but could only see the bright glow of the headlight. A dog ran out from a nearby courtyard and barked and chased the taxi for a moment, then quickly gave up.

Suddenly, the cycle kicked into a higher gear, the engine revving and screaming, and it rushed beside their taxi. Bob could see the outline of two people riding on it, and at first he thought it might be Tommy tracking him down with more news. But as soon as he glimpsed the two faces and then saw the man on the back raise up a piece of rebar in his hand, he yelled at the driver.

"Faster! Faster! Go!"

The driver looked at Bob as the man on the bike took his first swipe with the steel bar. He missed the window, but the heavy clang on the door caused the driver to jump in his seat. He swerved, and the edge of the taxi scraped against a stone wall. The man lifted his hand again, and this time he hit the window flush in the middle, shattering the glass. Bob covered his face.

"Go! Go!" he yelled. "Get out of here!"

"I no stuntman!" the driver yelled, and then the man on the back of the motorcycle grabbed the door and reached in, trying to unlock it. He jerked at it several times until it finally came free. He lunged at Bob, grabbing his ankle as Bob tried to kick him away. The taxi swerved down another alley and for a brief moment, separated from the cycle, but soon the driver of the motorcycle was next to them again, and the man on the back lifted one leg off the seat and tried to climb inside the taxi. Shards of broken glass flew off the seat around Bob's head as the taxi driver screamed and spun the wheel and slammed into the locked iron gate of a closed tailor shop. The taxi lurched to an abrupt stop, and the motorcycle skidded to a halt in front of them, then quickly turned around and came back to where they were. The man on the back leapt to the ground and ran to the broken rear door, reached in for Bob as Bob tried to pry his side of the door open, but it was jammed against the iron gate. The man grabbed Bob by the shoulder and began to drag him out of the taxi until, behind them, the sharp wail of a police siren suddenly ricocheted off the alley walls. A floodlight covered the taxi and the motorcycle in a blinding white glow. Through a loudspeaker, the driver of the police car shouted in Thai. The driver of the cycle looked back, then gunned the engine, and took off down the alley. The other man disappeared on foot, diving into the shadows of the dark streets.

The police cruiser pulled up beside Bob. In the backseat, a police captain, dressed in a dark gray uniform with a red sash over his shoulder, rolled down the window.

"You're welcome," he said.

Bob, who was still pinned against the rear door of the taxi, exhaled. "Manny," he said. "Thank you."

Captain Tanawat Sattaporn, or Manny as he liked to sometimes be called, motioned his hand forward. "Follow me."

****

The taxi pulled into the parking lot of the Wat Prayakrai Police Station. It was a mostly generic two-story cinder-block building except for the large oval portrait of the king and queen of Thailand that rose above the front entrance. Every station in the Royal Thai Police had one.

Bob gave the taxi driver his contact information and promised to pay for the damages. He followed Manny inside. Bob knew him well as he was the captain that oversaw the district where Saint Thomas had their offices. He had dealt with him when they first moved there and set everything up. Manny had been a big help with making sure they had all the correct licenses and permits, and he had never once stuck out his palm. Bob had never thought of him as an "eel," the term many Thai people used to refer to people in positions of authority; once in power they often became slippery, and one never knew what side they really stood on. Bob had always found Manny to be straight up, and he had also been a big help when their office had been burglarized last year.

They went to the second floor. Bob followed him to his desk and was about to sit down in a chair.

"No," said Manny. "In there." He motioned to one of the interrogation rooms.

Bob looked at him. "Are you serious?" Manny just stared

back. Bob held out his hands. "Do you want to cuff me as well?"

"In there," Manny said and lit a cigarette.

A Thai policeman escorted Bob inside the room, then shut the door. It was like most all such rooms. Nothing but a small steel table and two chairs. Bob sat down and waited. And waited. His neck began to ache.

Manny then entered the room, reading from a file folder, and sat down in front of Bob. He offered Bob a cigarette, but Bob shook his head no. Manny looked at Bob and smiled.

"British Catholics," he said.

"There's a few of us milling about," said Bob. Manny smiled again, and Bob did not like the look of that smile. In fact, he couldn't recall ever seeing Manny smile.

Manny studied Bob for several minutes. "How are you doing?"

"I'm fine. How are you? It's been a while."

"Did you have anything to do with the situation happening now at the embassy?"

"Manny, no. Of course not."

"Nothing?"

"No."

"You don't know any of the people involved?"

"No."

"You don't know a man who goes by the name Jonny?"

Bob hesitated. "No."

Manny waved his hand above his head. "Puffy hair. You never met him?"

"I met him briefly in Rangoon. I don't *know* him."

"Mm… You didn't hear any rumors?"

"I—I heard that maybe there was going to be a protest or something like that, but not this. What is going on there? What is the latest?"

"The latest is they want democracy in their country or they will soon start killing their hostages. One each hour. Just like that." Manny waved his hand. "They want democracy to magically appear, just like that. And you had nothing to do with this?"

Bob felt a sharp twinge in his neck. "No. Most certainly not."

Manny looked into his file again. "That was an interesting trip to Rangoon you had a few weeks ago."

"Yes, I—I shouldn't have done that."

"You are right," Manny said and smoked his cigarette. "You shouldn't have. You made a lot of people very angry. Here and there."

"Look, Manny—"

Manny interrupted Bob. "Tonight, you must call me Captain Sattaporn." No more smiles.

"Yes. I'm sorry. Captain, I—you know my history. I would never have been involved with anything where hostages or guns were involved."

"Yes, let's talk more about your history," said Captain Sattaporn as he turned a page in his file. "You are referring to Beirut. In 1985?"

Bob twirled his neck, trying to stop the growing pain. "Yes."

"Yes, that was tragic," continued the captain. "And then after that, you returned home to England in late 1986, was it? The following year you left the Catholic Church… I didn't know you could do that. You were not a priest for a few years? From 1987 to 1990?"

"Yes," Bob whispered. "That is correct."

"What happened to you?"

"You know what happened."

"Yes, Beirut, but I mean what happened to you those years when you weren't a priest? What did you do?"

Bob just sat there, the aching in his neck now spreading, swirling around his shoulder blades. "Captain—"

Manny took a photo from the file folder and placed it on the table. He turned it around so Father Bob could see it. It was a photo of a young boy with light-blond hair, dressed in a striped shirt and blue shorts. Bob began grinding his teeth.

"Gabriel Goodman. I like that name. But why is he not called Gabriel Hanlan? He is ten years old now? Mother, Sarah Goodman, living in Haverhill, England."

Bob just stared at the photo.

"I've been doing research," Captain Sattaporn continued. "About the Catholic Church and dispensations. The Internet is a wonderful thing. Too bad Y2K will soon destroy it. In order for you to enter the church again after a long absence, you had to be granted a dispensation. After what happened to you in Beirut, I'm sure they understood a crisis of confidence or faith could be explained. But I wonder, did they grant you a dispensation to become a priest again knowing you had fathered a child? Out of wedlock? In fact, that kind of dispensation has to come directly from the pope himself, correct?"

Bob squeezed the sides of his chair. "You are working for them, aren't you? Myanmar Intelligence. Where did you get all of this?"

Manny stood up and put out his cigarette on the edge of the table. "At this point, I am neither working for them nor against them. Just as at this point, I am neither protecting you nor letting you fend for yourself."

And there you have it, thought Bob. It had been a long con all along. Manny had been biding his time, waiting for the big score. Now he had it. "This is a bloody shakedown."

"This is not anything yet."

"Look at the clothes I'm wearing. I don't have much money. About four thousand sterling in savings and checking. One hundred and fifty thousand Thai baht. That's it. But I'm guessing that won't be enough, will it?"

Manny shook his head. "Not even. Saint Thomas Ministries Worldwide spends lots here in our country. Offices. Camps, vans."

"Yes, but I don't have any access or control over any of that. You know that."

"Yes, I supposed you would say that. Which is why I did more research and found out Gabriel Goodman's grandparents are Helen and Elliot Goodman. Both executives at the Royal Bank of Scotland. I'm sure they are well compensated? Or… I'm sure your superiors and your diocese back home would be extremely interested to hear about your extended family."

"I don't have any contact with them. That was the deal we agreed on. I didn't even know he was living in Haverhill until you just told me."

"Now you do know."

Bob took a deep breath in. "You bloody twat."

"Such strong language for a priest."

"I swore not to take the Lord's name in vain. I can still call you a dirty, corrupt motherfucker."

Manny walked toward Bob. He sat down on the edge of the table and loomed over the priest, Manny's breath a mixture of stale cigarette ash and cinnamon gum blowing into Bob's face. "A lot of people come here to Thailand to hide," Manny began. "They hide behind priest's collars, behind monk's robes, behind school walls, behind alcohol, and behind our women. And a lot of people never leave. They just *poof!...*" Manny held his fingers in front of his face and then popped them open as if letting go of a butterfly. "They just disappear." Captain Sattaporn smiled again. He pushed the photo over to Bob. "You can keep the picture. I have copies." He rose and gathered his file and opened the door. "I'll be in touch. Soon." He left the room.

Bob remained a few minutes before slowly rising. He put the photo in his jacket pocket. His neck and shoulders had tightened like a rubber band about ready to snap. He walked out the room, down the stairs, and out the front entrance. He briefly leaned against the front gate, then turned down Charoen Krung Road and began to walk back toward his home. For the first time in several days, he didn't look over his shoulder. At this point, he didn't care.

Part Two

Saturday, October 2, 1999

Broken glass constantly crunches and scrapes under the soles of their boots. The five rebel soldiers pace back and forth across the smoke and blood-stained tile floor in the lobby of the embassy. Death waits outside the tinted windows, stands beyond the white stone walls. But it has not come inside. There is fear stretched tight across the trembling faces of the twenty-three hostages corralled and lined-up on either side of the security desk, their bodies pressed against the fake wood walls. There is blood from cuts and scrapes that once dribbled across skin and fell upon the floor, but is now mostly dried into a dark red crust.

"Are you going to kill us?" a woman wearing a bright pink dress asks.

"Be patient," says Jonny, the man with the black, puffy hair.

"We believe the same as you," a man with a gray mustache says.

"Be patient," Jonny says.

He smashes the glass of a vending machine with the

end of his rifle and starts throwing bags of chips and candy at the people. Another soldier begins to cut the plastic ties from the hands and feet of each of the hostages. The driver of the truck, wearing a camouflage jumpsuit, brings in three cases of soda on a dolly and gives them to the people now rubbing away the red marks around their wrists and ankles. Jonny unwraps a Hershey's Bar, breaks it in half, and gives the pieces to the woman and the man he had been speaking with.

The phone at the security desk rings.

"They are calling again," says one of the soldiers. "The Thai police."

"Not yet," Jonny says. "We don't say anything."

He peers out the window at the night sky. There are no stars, the orange glow from the bright city lights a hazy blanket that covers them.

"Tomorrow," Jonny says. "We will speak to them tomorrow."

Chapter Ten

Michael Shaw woke to someone knocking on his door.

"Michael? Are you ok? It's Kat," said the light female voice from the hallway.

Michael rolled over slowly in his bed. The pink flowered sheets were an unholy mess, barely covering his naked body. A small patch of sunlight snuck through the curtains drawn around the patio doors. His eyes hurt and his mouth felt like sand.

"Kitty Kat?" he asked, clearing his throat several times.

"Yes. Can I come in?"

"Just a minute." Michael crawled to the floor and found his black sweat pants next to his desk. He nearly fell over putting each leg through them and then flopped back onto his mattress. "Ok. It's unlocked—I think… Come in."

Kitty Kat poked her head around the door, then entered the room. She was impeccably dressed as always. She wore a light-gray pantsuit with a striped button-up shirt that Michael thought looked great against her smooth almond-colored skin. It was good to see her. Her shiny black hair was cut short in a bob, and as she was a Thai Christian, she always wore a small gold cross on a chain around her neck. She was Michael's age, he knew, as he had gone to her birthday party two months ago. He could smell her clean, crisp scent as she came closer—simple and pure, like milk.

"Howdy, neighbor," Michael rasped.

She shuffled to the foot of Michael's bed. "Hey. Are you alright?"

"Mm... Just another day in paradise."

"I saw you last night when you got home. In the hallway. You probably don't remember."

Michael propped himself up on one arm. "I was pretty messed up, wasn't I?"

"Yes," said Kat. "Worse than usual." She then looked into the open doorway to his bathroom. "Michael, what did you do? What is going on?"

Michael turned his head and saw the bathroom floor covered in shattered glass. Silver shards from the mirror that now barely hung to the wall were mixed with dark-brown pieces from a smashed Singha beer bottle. Michael looked back at Kat with a blank face.

"I'll go get a broom. Do you need water? Food?"

"Water please," said Michael. "Thank you, Kitty Kat. You're the best."

She tried to smile. "You always say that."

Kat left the room. Michael tried to get out of bed, but a wave of nausea slammed him back down. He fought the urge, swallowing hard until it passed, and then images from the night before began to come back to him: the go-go bars, the dark cubicle, the girl with too much makeup, lying on the sidewalk across from Lumphini Park, crying, wailing, screaming. He then remembered walking home, stopping off at JK Foods just as it was closing, and Miss Nona putting two more bottles of beer in plastic bags. Coming back here, drinking more, spinning around naked in his room, then shouting, "Enough!" and hurling a bottle against the mirror in the bathroom. So dramatic. So pathetic.

Kitty Kat came back in and gave Michael a cold bottle of water. He took slow sips and watched her. There was both a simple elegance and a charming clumsiness in the way she moved, her small frame gliding like a young swan learning how to walk. She took a broom and dustbin into his bathroom and began to sweep up his mess. Often, pieces of glass flew to the side and missed her intended target.

When Michael first moved here, Father Bob had introduced them, and the first few weeks they had spent a lot of time together. She had acted like a tour guide, showing him the sights and tastes of Bangkok. Their first day out on the town, she took him to the Grand Palace, the mesmerizing gold domes, the never-ending layers of roofs and archways, roaming together barefoot over the intricate tiled floors. She knew all about the history of every place they went. Her English was flawless, probably better than his. He found out she was a teacher at a pricey private international school not far from their apartment building, and over their first lunch together, dim sum and lemongrass soup at a tiny but sparkling little dive in Chinatown, Kat had confessed to him that a few years ago she had once been engaged, but her fiancé had died suddenly from meningitis. She now lived alone in the apartment two doors down from him.

Over the days that followed, she took him to see the statue of the Emerald Buddha, smaller than he'd thought, but still stunning as she explained it was decorated in its rainy season attire of a pointed headpiece, gold studded with sapphires, and a gold-embossed monk's robe draped over one shoulder. They took several boat trips down the Chao Phraya River, sometimes crossing over to the western bank and exploring the shopping districts of Chom Thong, quieter and more open-air without the crush of high-rise buildings, full of similar kinds of food and knock-off designer clothes he could find along Silom Road, but as it was off the main tourist drag, you could get a more *local* price. One night they went to an outdoor jazz concert in Lumphini Park, the lush, green oasis, Bangkok's version of Central Park; but by far his favorite moment with her had been the evening they spent at the floating market. She had brushed against his body four times.

One: They strolled along the *klongs,* the black-ink water canals, where all the vendors bobbed up and down in their longboats full of vegetables and fruit and fried meat or fried fish. It was a swirling, vibrant scene with so many colors and scents and noises. She would point to each boat and explain what they were selling, where the people came from, and as they stood along the dock in front of a woman wearing a bamboo paddy hat and selling freshly grilled pineapple, Kat leaned over and brushed her leg against his.

Two: They walked along the riverbank in the late afternoon holding popsicles of frozen mango slices, and she stumbled just a bit, reached out to grab his shoulder to steady herself, and allowed her feet to tangle up within his.

Three: After the market closed, they joined hundreds of others along the waterside, as they lit small candles covered by gossamer paper called wish lanterns. The lanterns floated into the sky, hundreds of them like square fireflies, a domino effect of yellow-orange rectangles drifting over the river. At that moment, the back of her hand pressed directly against his, gingerly waiting for their fingers to open up and merge together. But Michael hesitated, and the moment passed.

The fourth and final brush against his body came as they arrived back home to their building. They entered the elevator, and she pressed her shoulder against his arm as she reached over to push the button to their sixth floor. He sucked in her clean, milky scent. It sent a rush of hot blood through his body. He wanted her. Yes, he really wanted her but...

He walked her to her door, and she invited him in for tea and to watch a video. She had told him she loved old Hollywood films from the '50s and '60s—anything with Grace Kelly, Cary Grant, Jimmy Stewart, or Audrey Hepburn—and she had a dozen tapes Michael could choose from. *Yes,* thought Michael, as she stood in her doorway. He looked into her upturned face, her clean, light-brown skin and watched her chest breathe up and down underneath her purple cotton blouse. He wanted to go inside and wrap himself around her, but at the same time, he wanted to run back to his room, alone. She was so smart, so pretty. He was a roiling caldron of toxic acid. She had an enormous smile, and Michael now knew, she had a great heart as well. She was exactly the type of woman he *should* be spending time with, but exactly the kind he now most avoided; because at that moment, watching her chest rise and fall, despite how much he wanted to see her body rise and fall from the bed they might share together, he couldn't do it. He would scald her, he would poison her; it wouldn't be fair.

"I'm a bit tired tonight. Also, I'll be busy the next few days. Maybe next week?"

"Sure," Kat had said. "Sure…"

Michael walked down the hallway alone, leaving Kat with her head bowed, standing by her door.

****

Kat shook the broken glass into a paper bag. She then came over and sat down on the edge of Michael's bed. "When is the last time you ate?"

"I don't know. I need to diet anyway. Getting fat."

"It's not food that's making you fat."

"Touché."

Kat sighed out. "Michael, what are you doing?"

"Trying to wake up."

"You know what I mean."

Michael looked at the crooked bathroom mirror, hanging on its last hinge. "Yes. I do."

"You're better than this."

"I'm not so sure."

"Stop it," said Kat emphatically. "You are... Whatever you are hiding from, whatever you are trying to forget, it's not working, is it?"

Michael took a sip of water. "No... It definitely isn't."

Kat tangled her fingers together, pressing them and squeezing them. "So many Western men come here and commit slow suicide."

Michael squirmed in the bed. She was always dead-on, always saw right through him, more than anyone he had met.

"You don't need to do that," she said softly. "I told you I could get you a teaching job at my school. They pay well. They are nice people. But not like this. Not the way you are now."

"I understand."

Kat reached out for the bottle of water, and Michael passed it to her. She took a sip. "I haven't seen much of you lately."

"Please don't take it personally. I've been that way with

everyone."

She handed the water back to Michael. "Some of the other teachers and myself are planning a day-trip to Ayutthaya. It's kind of our version of Angkor Wat. Only a forty-minute train ride. You should come. It would be good to get out of the city."

"Sounds good. Maybe next week?"

"Sure," said Kat. "Next week…"

They sat a moment in silence. The air conditioner cut on and whirred to life. Kat moved as if to stand up, but Michael reached out and grabbed her arm to stop her. "I'm sorry. I didn't use to be like this."

"I'm sure," said Kat.

Her voice, her calm presence, was like a magnet sucking out the rotten metal inside him. He suddenly burst out. "Fuck! I don't know what's happening to me… Kat, I used to have my act together. I really did. Believe me! Then… I just don't know. Over the past couple of years, it all started falling apart. Stupid decisions. Dumb moves. Things I never, ever thought I would have done. Just stupid. Sinking deeper. Shrinking away… I keep thinking I can stop all this and be that person again. The one I used to be before all this. Who had so much promise, who had so much going for him. I just… I just…"

Kat twirled her gold cross in her fingers. "Feel better?" she asked.

A deep sigh rushed out from inside him. "A bit," said Michael.

"How about just not being the person you are right now? Start with that."

Michael quietly nodded.

Kat took her thumb, licked it, and pressed it against Michael's forehead. "You need to speak to someone. There's obviously a lot going on in that head of yours."

Michael wrapped his hand around hers and pressed her thumb even tighter against his skin. "You mean like a shrink?"

"Maybe... Or how about Father Bob?"

Michael let go and looked at the circle of sunlight on the floor in front of his curtains. "As usual, you've read my mind. I've thought of that."

"He's a good man. A wise man. He likes to help people."

"I will."

"How about today? You should probably see him anyway about what's going on at the embassy."

"The embassy?"

"You haven't heard? A group of rebels took over the Burmese

embassy yesterday. They took all personnel hostage. It's been all over the news."

"Self-absorbed as usual. Was it my group, the Mon?"

"No. Students, maybe led by the Karen. They have threatened to start shooting hostages if they don't get their homeland recognized. It's been crazy down there. Can't get anywhere within a kilometer. Thai military is everywhere."

"Christ. I missed all that. Yes, I'll go see him today."

"You promise?"

"I do, Kitty Kat. I do." Michael and Kat paused a moment and looked into each other's faces. *Clean. She is so clean.* "We should get married," Michael suddenly said. A moment of silence, then both burst out laughing.

Kat's eyes sparkled and glistened, and her huge smile perfectly framed her petite face. She bit her bottom lip and locked eyes with Michael again. "Maybe. Someday… but not now. Not like this."

"I don't blame you," said Michael. He then leaned over and kissed her cheek. He took a deep breath, sucking in her fresh scent. "You are the best, Kitty Kat. And I really do mean that."

"I know. And thank you." Kat reached out and squeezed Michael's hand, then stood up, grabbed the broom and paper bag, and walked toward the door.

"So, Ayutthaya next week?" she asked.

"Next week. I promise," said Michael.

"Good," said Kat. "Please take it easy."

"I will," said Michael. "For you."

"For yourself," she said. Kitty Kat smiled, blew Michael a kiss, and then left the room.

****

Michael opened the curtains to his patio. There across the road was the palm tree, rising high and looking as green and as full as ever. The recent rains seemed to have given it new power. Michael then remembered he had made it home last night just as a storm broke and how he had stood out on his balcony well past midnight, beer in one hand, holding the wet railing with his other, and leaning out as far as he could, six stories up, trying to catch raindrops in his mouth. Another brilliant move. Below the tree, on the corner of his street was the soup cart he liked, and he decided the first thing was getting food. He had had nothing to eat since those chicken breasts yesterday morning. He put on some cargo shorts and a white T-shirt and slipped on his sandals. In the lobby, Sherri was nowhere to be found, so he was able to make it outside without incident.

An elderly Thai woman known as Miss Trisha worked at the cart every day from early morning until late at night. A pot of constantly boiling water stood in the center of the cart, and then rising next to it were four glass shelves packed with all the ingredients you could choose. Michael pointed out a clump of thin rice noodles, and Miss Trisha dropped them in the boiling water. Then he asked for the small meatball-sized, white and tan fish balls and pork balls, which were sweet, soft, salty, and delicious though he still didn't know exactly what they were made of. Next he asked for bok choy, water spinach, and carrots. It only took about two minutes in the boiling pot for all the ingredients to cook, and then Trisha scooped everything out into a large plastic bowl, added some beef stock and fish sauce, and carried it all over to one of the four small yellow plastic tables under an umbrella along the sidewalk. A wire cart of different sauces and condiments was on each table, and Michael scooped out some of the sweet and spicy chili sauce, which turned the soup a red color. He took the chopsticks, clamped down on a big pile of vegetables and noodles, steadying his hand a bit as it shook, and put it in his mouth. It was so good. It was his favorite food in all of Bangkok.

After he finished, he lit a cigarette with his orange plastic lighter and sat at the table awhile, thinking. He saw himself again lying on the sidewalk last night and remembered the sharp pain in his stomach, like something inside clawing to get out; Kitty Kat this morning and the way she smelled; broken glass on his bathroom floor. Next door to the soup cart was a stop-n-shop store, and a cooler of Chang Beer jutted out onto the sidewalk. He imagined how cold it was. He looked at his watch: 9:00 a.m. Not much earlier than when he usually began drinking each day. It would be very easy to do. Very familiar. Very comfortable.

And very stupid. He had to start somewhere. As Kitty Kat so wisely had said, "Stop being the person you are right now." He was staring at the magical fork in the road. He could go this way, or that. It was time to fish or cut bait. Shit or get off the pot—and all the other overused phrases he couldn't think of at this moment.

Michael stood up and hailed a taxi, telling the driver to take him to Charoen Rat Road.

Chapter Eleven

The TV had been on in Father Bob's house all morning since he woke at 5:00 a.m. The best coverage came from the local Thai station, and according to their reporters, negotiators had been speaking with the rebels all through the night, and it now appeared their demands had changed to just getting out alive. They were demanding transport across the border back to Burma. As of yet, none of the hostages had been reported hurt or dead. Images showed the Thai military now completely surrounding the white walls of the embassy, which was a fitting metaphor, he thought, for after his confrontation with Manny last night, it seemed everything else in his life right now had him completely surrounded as well—from all sides, with no place to go. Myanmar wanted him. Manny wanted him. Father Timothy wanted nothing to do with him. The Karen rebels had used him. And now that lovely, innocent boy in Haverhill, England, his mother Sarah, who since childhood had been one of

Bob's closest friends, and now even her own family, were all being drawn into this ugly, careless quagmire Bob had created for himself.

Still, he had work to do. Just keep moving, and try to figure it all out later. Around 7:00 that morning, one of the novice monks from Wat Prok had knocked on his door and hand delivered a note from Pra Tissa saying that he and Pra Ramanya wanted to speak to him privately about an urgent matter. He was impressed with how good their English was now. The American lad Michael had been doing a cracking job, and it was just as he was preparing to leave when another knock came from his door. He peeked out from his curtains, surprised and relieved to see Michael himself standing on his steps.

Bob slowly peeled open the door. "Michael? How odd. I was just thinking about you."

"Really?"

"Yes." Bob took a quick scan around the alley to see if anyone else was lurking about. All seemed clear. "Sorry. Come in, come in."

Michael took off his shoes, then heard the TV reports coming from Bob's living room. "Is that about the embassy? I just heard about it this morning." Michael moved toward it and saw images of the Thai military on the streets and helicopters hovering overhead.

"Yes. Bloody mess. So far at least no one seems to have been hurt. I've still got a warm kettle if you want some tea. Sorry, no coffee. I know how you Yanks love that in the morning."

Michael still stared at the television. "No thanks, I'm fine. So none of our group, the Mon, they aren't involved are they?"

"No," said Bob. "But this will affect them. There will be blowback with all the refugees when this is said and done."

"Did you know about this?"

Bob took a deep breath and bit down on his back teeth. "So how can I help you?"

Michael pulled his eyes away from the images. "Oh. Yes. I... I was wondering if you had some time to talk. Privately."

Bob watched Michael's eyes move around the room, avoiding looking directly at him. He liked the lad but upon first meeting him months ago, had picked up on a strong sense of sadness, a definite lost-in-the-woods quality. And now seeing Michael's red, puffy face and his watery eyes, he began to get a clearer image of what could be going on. "Of course, Michael. I'd be happy to talk. How about this afternoon? You could come by our office. I'm the only one there. Everyone else is out at Chiang Mai."

"Um, sure. That would be ok."

"I was actually just getting ready to head over to the temple. Tissa sent me a note this morning that he and Ramanya wanted to

116

speak to me."

"Really? Ramanya missed most of class yesterday. He said he was sick. Did they say what it was about?"

"No. Just that it was urgent." Bob watched Michael standing in the middle of his living room, fidgeting with his keys. "By the way, their English has gotten so much better. You are really doing a great job. They say you are the best teacher they've ever had."

"Thanks. I really enjoy it. They are great people."

Bob put his breakfast cups and dishes in the sink. Yes indeed, a razor-sharp picture about what was probably troubling the lad now came into focus. He had seen that shattered look before many times, on many people. "Hey, I've got a capital idea. Why don't you come with me? To the temple," said Bob.

"Now?"

"Sure. They would love to see you. Then we can talk afterward. Maybe get lunch somewhere."

Michael thought a moment. The image of his dark, quiet room flashed in his mind. Sitting on the floor. Cold beer going down his throat, to his head. It pulled at him. It taunted him… Fish or cut bait…

"Yes. I'll go. Thanks for asking."

"Great. We'll walk to the main road and get a bike taxi." Bob turned off the TV, grabbed his wallet and keys, then the two of them left the house and headed down the alley. The storm the night before had actually left a slight chill to the morning air, which compared to daily Bangkok weather, was refreshing and unexpected. A giant puddle covered almost the entire pavement, and Bob and Michael skirted around the edge, the tips of their shoes just dipping in and getting wet.

"How much longer will the rainy season last?" asked Michael.

"About a week or two more," said Bob. He looked up at a window from one of the houses to see the young boy Hank staring down at him. Bob waved at the boy, and a big smile crept across the child's face.

"I actually kind of like it," said Michael. "Seems to help with the pollution."

"Yes, this year hasn't been too bad. In the past, there have been huge floods. There is a reptile farm at the north edge of the city, and a couple of years ago huge rains flooded it, and all the animals escaped. There were crocs and snakes and giant lizards swimming and crawling all over the streets for days. It was mental. As if this city isn't mad enough without having to dodge a crocodile while crossing the street."

"Yeah. It's quite intense here, to be sure."

"Are you enjoying yourself?" Bob asked and carefully watched Michael's face.

"Well, yes. I mean the people are great. Thais are so friendly. And the food is amazing. And I love working with the monks…"

Bob knew enough not to push it at this moment. "Yes, a fascinating country. It's easy to get swept up in it all."

"Uh… yes."

They arrived at the intersection to the main road and the motorcycle stand. Only one boy was there, and Bob couldn't remember his name, but he, of course, knew Bob.

"Tommy back soon," said the boy.

"Let's wait a bit," Bob said to Michael. Bob then looked back down the alley again, always feeling like he would turn around and see more shadows following him. He wondered if Manny himself wasn't running the whole operation. Probably getting a nice chunk of change from Myanmar Intelligence to keep tabs on him, and maybe even a bounty was involved as well. "Father Bob Hanlan: Myanmar's Most Wanted. Dead or Alive." Bob conjured up a poster in his mind, trying to make light of the situation. It didn't work. He also wasn't sure if Manny hadn't actually staged the whole event with the taxi last night as well, just to get his attention and put extra pressure on him. It didn't matter. Either way Manny was now very dangerous, and Bob shuddered at how quickly one could turn from ally to enemy.

Tommy came roaring to a stop on his motorbike. He took off his helmet and smiled at Bob. "Bollocks! Bollocks! Father Bob!"

Bob rolled his eyes. "Hello, Tommy. I should have never taught you that."

"It's fun! Where are you going?"

"We need to go to Wat Prok. Both of us."

"Ok. The road up there is no good. Bad traffic. We have to take long way. By river."

"The scenic route. How fortunate." He turned to Michael. "You taken a motorcycle taxi before?"

"Once," said Michael, raising his eyebrows.

Bob smiled in understanding. "I used to hate it as well. Now it's the only way I like to travel. Don't worry. These kids will take good care of us."

They each climbed on the back of their bikes, Bob wrapping his arms around Tommy and Michael around the other driver.

Tommy revved his engine a few times. "Here we go!"

****

With a pop and a swerve, both bikes took off, barreling down the never-ending, claustrophobic maze of side streets and alleyways that spread like tangled roots off all the main avenues in Bangkok. It seemed like ten streets all had the same name, as they tilted in and out of Yudi Alley, Yu Di Alley, Charoen Rat 7 Yeak 7, Charoen Rat 7 Yeak 6-7, Sut Prasoet Alley, and Sut Prasoet Alley 2/1. Ramshackle homes and teetering townhouses, with tin for roofs and rusty sheets of corrugated steel for fences, flew past them, and the occasional sharp lean of the cycle sent a curdling reminder in Michael's stomach of all the booze he had pummeled his body with the night before.

Finally, they burst open into free space, turning on the wide boulevard known as Charoen Krung road. The gorgeous Chao Phraya River was to their left as they headed north. The waves of the water bounced energetically under the wide glistening sky, and the sky itself around them seemed brighter and sharper, the rainy season having scrubbed the air clean, washing away the usual polluted haze. The crisp sunlight lit up all the colors. There seemed to be endless space, infinite directions they could go as Michael now realized just how dark and imprisoned his world had been these past several weeks. The river was only about a mile from his apartment, yet he had forgotten it even existed. Zoom, zoom up the boulevard, as taxis, buses, and *tuk-tuks* rushed past them. Bangkok was booming; there was no fear of the coming apocalypse in this town as cranes poked everywhere in the sky, raising up new office buildings, luxury apartments, hotels, and shopping centers. The tall stone pillars of the coming SkyTrain—the elevated commuter train that promised to revolutionize the way people traveled in this city—were growing from sidewalks. Add to all of that the sprawling parade of food carts and their collection of red, yellow, blue plastic tables and chairs. The swirling Thai script letters of all the signs, the overflowing sidewalk markets with spiky lychees, bulbous swollen jackfruits and durians, fuzzy red rambutans, mangoes, papayas, lemongrass, ginger, Thai chilies, water spinach, and holy basil.

The two bikes ran side by side, and Bob looked over at Michael, then took his hands off Tommy's waist and threw them in the air—"No hands, man!"—tilting his head back, laughing, and Michael tried to follow, first one arm then the other, and then the air seemed to lift him up, up, up off the seat until he was flying through the big blue sky.

Chapter Twelve

Ramanya sat on the floor, alone, in the *bot*, the most sacred worship room at Wat Prok. It was somewhat sparse in comparison to other temples: a bronze statue of the Buddha rose about three meters off the floor. Thin white curtains covered the walls behind it, and thin strings of white and lavender electric lights draped down from the ceiling. The floor was smooth, stone, and cool to the touch.

　　"Buddham saranam gacchami (I go for refuge in the Buddha)

　　Dhammam saranam gacchami (I go for refuge in the Dharma)

　　Sangham saranam gacchami (I go for refuge in the Sangha)"

　　Ramanya repeated these phrases three times, just as he had done sixteen months ago when first ordained as a monk at the temple. Reaffirmation and guidance were what he now desperately sought. He opened his eyes and stared at the statue. For a moment there was pure silence in the room—no sound at all came from beyond the walls—no car horns, no dogs barking, and no wind. Then, as in his dream, his mother's voice crept into his ears. It was as if she were sitting next to him, and it tore his chest apart with a deep longing to curl up in her lap like he had done when he was a child. He closed his eyes again and tried several different chants, but each time he was unable to truly focus. There was just too much chaos swirling in his head, and he didn't yet have the discipline or experience to conquer it. Ramanya stood up and slowly walked out the room. He knew today he would have to make his decision.

Tissa had been waiting patiently outside the entrance. "They're here," he said to Ramanya.

"They?"

"Michael is here as well."

The two old friends crossed the courtyard, under the shadows of the multitier, spiky rooftops, and ascended the narrow staircase to the open-air classroom on the top floor. Michael and Bob stood up and clasped their hands in front of their faces and bowed their heads. All four settled into desks arranged in a small circle. Below them, the sounds of children playing soccer in the cemetery rose up from the ground and filled the air as Ramanya recounted to Father Bob and Michael all that had transpired over the past day. When he finished,

Ramanya stood up and began to slowly pace around the circular edge of the room. Bob folded his chin in his hands and remained silent.

Michael didn't quite understand it all. "Wait. So you were a soldier? In Burma?"

"Show him the photos," Ramanya said to Tissa.

"We both were," said Tissa. "In the Mon Rebel Army." Tissa reached under a fold in his saffron robe and pulled out a tattered envelope. He took out a small stack of photographs and spread them on the desk. Michael stood up and walked over to see them.

"Son of a bitch," he said, then quickly caught himself. "Sorry," he said.

"It's ok," said Tissa. Tissa pointed at one of himself in full camouflage, sitting outside a small thatched hut. "That's me. I was a captain…" Then he took out a photo of a slender man with thick black hair and long bushy sideburns, olive army cap resting on his head. The man was smiling. "And that was Ramanya."

"Holy Christ—sorry."

"It's ok," said Tissa patiently.

"So… The two of you were fighting? Against the Myanmar Army? The government?"

"I'm sad to say, yes," said Tissa. Ramanya continued to slowly pace around the room, and Bob watched silently. "It has been going on for years, for centuries," said Tissa. "The Mon are our own people. We lived on our land for nearly a millennium before there was ever any country called Burma or Myanmar. Just like the Karen. We have our own language. Our own customs. Yet the current leaders won't allow us to follow them."

"Worse," said Ramanya. "They come to our villages. They take our people and force them to work as slaves in their army. Building roads, cleaning sewers, getting little food, no medicine, and if they die, so be it. They toss us on the side of the road like dead rats."

"This has been going on all our lives," said Tissa. "Ramanya and I grew up together, and together we decided to join the rebel army when we were just teenagers."

Michael looked at Bob, but Bob continued to clutch his chin in silence. "So... have you... Have you killed people?" asked Michael.

Tissa looked over at Ramanya. Ramanya stopped pacing, then walked over and stood behind Tissa's chair. "I was a munitions expert," said Ramanya. "They called me the bomb-maker. The Black Fox. So yes. I have."

Michael sat down on the edge of the table in front of the chalkboard. "You knew about all this?" he asked Bob. Bob simply raised his eyebrows and shifted in his seat.

Ramanya continued. "Two years ago, we got word of a forest meeting of several of the Myanmar generals in charge of wiping out our *kind*. It was at an old Japanese war camp. Five officers and six infantrymen spent two days planning, we assumed, new assaults against our people. The second night, I crawled through the underbrush and set charges all around the main barracks where they slept. I did my job well. At 3:25 a.m., the explosives went off and all eleven were killed."

Michael's mouth froze wide open.

"Then two months later," Tissa said, "the government raided our village, pulled everyone they could find into the central square, shot them, burned their bodies, burned all houses to the ground."

"It was because of me this happened," said Ramanya. "It was vengeance. My mother and sister were in that pile of bodies. Or so I had thought until yesterday."

Tissa chimed in. "And now this man suddenly appears saying he can bring Ramanya to his family, his family who have been in hiding all this time. For sixteen months. With no prior word."

"Brother—" Ramanya gently rebuked Tissa.

"I'm sorry. I know you so badly want to, but I just don't believe this is true. This is just a trick for the military to get you home and string you up and skin you alive. They will stop at nothing until you are dead. They will stick your head on a pike!"

Father Bob finally stood up and held out his hand to referee. "Ok. All right. Emotions are high. There is a lot to consider. Let's step back a bit and walk ourselves through it." Now it was he who paced around the circular rim of the room.

"Don't go, Ramanya," said Tissa.

Bob stood front and center at the chalkboard. He breathed in deep, then sighed out. "Ok, thank you, Tissa. Ramanya, do you believe this man who came to you? What does your instinct tell you?"

"I believe him," said Ramanya. Tissa shook his head, stood up, and moved to the far edge of the room.

"Ok, Tissa, I understand you are skeptical, but let's think this through," said Bob.

"Why now?" asked Tissa. "Really? On the same day the embassy is attacked?"

"Yes, that is the other big issue," said Bob. "It won't be long, tomorrow, maybe even one more day, before the Myanmar military moves in and completely seals the border."

"Yes," said Ramanya. "We can't go through the main checkpoint at Three Pagodas Pass, but now at the end of the rainy season, there are several temporary creeks and swells along the border I can cross at night before the army moves in."

"Tomorrow night at the latest would be your last chance," said Bob.

"Miss Sally," said Ramanya.

"Exactly," said Bob. "Miss Sally."

Michael felt like whiplash was breaking his neck, trying to keep up with the rapid-fire discussion. "Miss Sally?"

"She's a Thai national, but Mon sympathizer," said Bob. "She runs a private boarding house on the Thai-Burma border, as well as kind of an underground railway for refugees and smugglers."

"Smugglers? Seriously?" said Michael.

"She's kind of like an Asian Harriet Tubman," said Bob.

"Couldn't you just bring them here?"

"It's too dangerous. And expensive," said Ramanya. "They don't have any money. When Tissa and I came over, we had to sell all of our weapons to pay the passage fees. They have nothing to get money. Plus my sister is only eleven years old. This man told me they are in a safe place and being protected carefully."

Tissa strode up and wrapped his forearm behind Ramanya's neck. "Brother, if you choose this, you are on your own. I will not go with you. You and I renounced that life sixteen months ago. We came here to break that cycle of violence. We took vows. We are not here just hiding out. We made a commitment to change our lives. We made a commitment toward peace. I'm not going back. My life is here now. My life there is dead."

"I understand, brother," said Ramanya. "But it appears, despite all our best efforts, my life there is still very much alive."

Tissa took his arms from around Ramanya. All four stopped moving.

"Ramanya," asked Bob. "What do you want to do?"

Ramanya pressed his palm under his chin and clamped down on his jaw. He turned around and looked at the wide expanse of the Bangkok skyline, then down below at the people milling about in the Chinese cemetery. He turned back around to find his friends and colleagues staring at him, waiting. Ramanya then planted both feet firmly on the floor of the classroom, let his arms drop gently by his side, and closed his eyes. To Michael, it was almost like an optical illusion as Ramanya seemed to become completely immobile, transforming into a statue before his eyes. There didn't even appear to be any breaths coming from his body, but inside Ramanya's mind, he retraced, for the thousandth time, all the events that had brought him to this moment, especially the dream he had had, the dream that had taken place in this very room, the white cat, his mother's voice swirling all around him, and then that great noise again rose up, the deep humming that turned into a heavy pounding and rumbling that grew louder and more violent until all at once it stopped.

Ramanya opened his eyes. "I need to go," he said.

Tissa collapsed into a chair and stared at the floor. "I'm sorry, brother," said Ramanya. "But if there is even the slightest chance they are alive, I have to go. How could I ever find peace here knowing that?"

For several moments, no one spoke further, then Bob said: "I'll go with you."

"You don't need to," said Ramanya.

"I want to," said Bob. "But we will have to leave today. Soon. We won't be able to make it all the way to the border tonight, but we can stop off in Kanchanaburi and try to contact Miss Sally from there. Saint Thomas has a camp there where we can spend the night."

"Yes, I must go there anyway," said Ramanya. "To Wat Varman. I have two children there I have sponsored. I need to see them one last time before I go."

"There's a 1:10 train leaving from Thonburi Station, just over two hours from now, the last of the day. That will get us there late afternoon."

"Can we not take one of the vehicles from Saint Thomas?" asked Ramanya.

"They are all away at Chiang Mai. Plus, I can't drive anyway. I don't have a license."

"Really?" Michael chimed in.

"Yes. Drive in this city? Must be mad. Do you have one?"

"Well. For South Carolina. Not here."

"So train it is."

Tissa continued to stare at the floor and not speak. Bob walked over to him and placed his hand on his shoulder. "I promise. I'll do my best to take care of him."

"It's not you who I'm worried about," said Tissa.

Ramanya placed his hand on Tissa's other shoulder, then turned toward Bob. "I need to go get medicine and supplies for the children."

"Yes, I have a few things to do as well. So I'll meet you at the station?"

Ramanya nodded. He and Michael and Father Bob slowly moved toward the stairs. Tissa remained in the chair, not looking at any of them. Ramanya looked back at him once more, then disappeared down the staircase.

Chapter Thirteen

Bob had offered to walk Michael back to his apartment. Neither of them spoke a word during the ten-minute journey. When they entered the lobby, Sherri was there.

"Father Bob! So good to see you. It has been awhile. Are you taking good care of my favorite boy, Michael?" Sherri said and walked with them.

"Yes, Sherri, I wouldn't have it any other way."

"Yes, so nice. Friends are so nice. If there is anything I can do for you, please ask?"

"Of course. No one else in the world I could think of."

Sherri smiled and waved as the two entered the elevator and the doors shut. Inside Bob turned to Michael. "She's cute," he said and gave Michael a wink. Michael shook his head and both laughed.

Once inside Michael's apartment, Michael pulled out a Fanta Lemon soda from his mini fridge. He offered to split it into two cups, but Bob politely refused. Michael slipped off his sandals and sat on the edge of his bed. Bob walked around the room then stopped when he saw the broken mirror on the bathroom wall. He looked on the floor and saw a single piece of brown glass from the broken beer bottle.

He turned around and motioned with his eyes toward the bathroom. "So, is this what you wanted to talk to me about?" he asked.

"Yes," said Michael.

"How long has this been a problem?"

"How long? Well, I don't know. I guess it kind of started a couple of years ago but…"

"But now it's grown into something much worse?"

"Yes. I think so."

Bob sighed and took a seat in the chair next to Michael's desk. "So let me then ask you this: is this just a symptom of something else bothering you, or is it its own problem?"

"I don't know. I really don't anymore."

"Well, I'm not qualified to make those types of judgments.

You would need to see a professional. Maybe even consider checking into a facility."

"You mean like rehab?"

"Yes. If you've really reached this point. I've known several who have gone through this. Most have to reach rock bottom before they can start to turn things around."

"I think I have. Last night."

"Hmm… Well, there is a public clinic here in Bangkok, but I don't think you want to go there. It's pretty hard-core. Cuckoo's nest. There are a couple of private clinics that cater to *farangs* such as ourselves, but they are not free. Not nearly as expensive as those in the States, but not free."

"What do you think?"

Bob took a moment, carefully looked at Michael. He looked around the room and how sparse and empty and downright gloomy it was. "I think you should go home."

"To the States?"

"Yes."

"I can't."

"Can't or don't want to?"

"Both," said Michael. "It's complicated."

"It always is," said Bob.

"You don't want me to continue working with the monks?"

"No, that's not it at all. You are doing a wonderful job. They really love you."

"I take it seriously. I really give my best."

"I know you do. You are a great teacher but… A person can be many different things all at once. Even if you go to a clinic, there is no 'cure.' You are never cured. It's something that will be with you the rest of your life. You need a good support system. Family and friends are important."

Michael took a sip of his lemon soda. "I'll think about it."

"Ok. I'm here to help you any way I can. I mean that."

"I know. And thank you."

Bob nodded, then stood up. "Sorry, but I need to get a few things done before I go to the station."

Suddenly the dark images of this room filled Michael's head, of him sitting here alone like had done most every single day. But this time they didn't taunt him. They disgusted him.

"Can I go with you?" he blurted out.

"Where? To the station?"

"With you and Ramanya. To wherever it is you're going. Please, I can't stay here alone anymore. I need to get out. I need to do something. I need to help him. I want to help him."

"Michael…" Bob looked at the desperate, jagged expression wrapped around Michael's face. A violent torrent of pain and confusion. Bob's first impulse was to say no, but then something deeper tugged at him. How could Bob now not reach out to him? Wasn't this exactly what his whole manic life had been about? Helping people? Anytime. Anywhere. Anyway necessary?

"I can't have you getting snockered," said Bob.

"I won't. I promise. No booze."

"No, that won't work either. If you've really arrived at the place you say you have, going cold turkey is just as bad. You have to keep it steady for the next couple of days. Until we get back. Then I'll look into maybe helping you get into one of the private clinics here. Maybe we can work out a deal where you pay me back whenever you can."

"Yes, I could get more teaching jobs. I could do that."

Bob thought a moment more. "Train leaves in two hours."

"Thank you. Thank you so much."

He reached out and grabbed Michael by the forearm. "We'll figure this out," said Bob, and then he left the room.

Michael lit a cigarette. He stood up and paced around his apartment, then looked out the glass doors of the patio. Everything he saw on this blue-collar street was continuing on its usual rhythm—the food carts, the mechanics, the construction workers, the teenagers lounging in the snooker halls—all went about their daily routine; but he felt a bit different. Inside him he felt a promising flicker that maybe this day, this moment, would be looked back on in his own life as the first turning point, as the first tiny moment when things finally began to change. Michael looked up and saw the glowing, green palm tree swaying gently in the wind. It seemed to fill the entire sky.

Chapter Fourteen

Bob walked around the giant puddle on Yudi Alley, looked up at his front door, and saw something metallic and silver flashing in the sun. As he got closer, the image of a switchblade jammed into the wood of his door became clear. The knife had pinned a small note to the frame. The note was handwritten in red ink. It said simply: SOON. Bob tore off the paper and left the knife stuck there as he went inside.

Bob walked into his bedroom and took out a small daypack and began to fill it with clothes. What did Manny expect to happen "SOON"? Bob surmised Manny expected to get paid, one way or the other. Either Bob agreed to his terms of blackmail, or Manny would turn Bob over to the Myanmar goon squad and collect his bounty that way. Or perhaps first Manny would torture his prey a bit by exposing his secret to Father Timothy and the others. Bob could see and hear Father Timothy now rattling off the list of church canons he had violated: canon 290: once ordained to be a priest, it never becomes invalid, even when attempting to remove oneself from one's duties; canon 291: even when a priest loses the clerical state, it is not a dispensation from the requirement to stay celibate; canon 1394.1; canon 194.n.3; canon 1087, etc., etc., etc....

He didn't even know how to get in touch with Sarah or her family, but Bob was sure Manny had done his homework for him. Regardless, no time for that now. He'd have to deal with it when he got back. Maybe he could even try meeting with Manny again. Speak to him. Reason with him. Try to rediscover that helpful person he had known the previous six years... maybe.

Bob gathered up everything he needed for his trip and stopped by the mirror in the hallway. "Curry and snow... Time to go," he said. He took a step out his front door, then quickly went back to the kitchen. He opened up his pantry, took out a jar of peanut butter, grabbed a spoon from his drawer, and dropped it into his backpack. He then went outside and locked all the bolts to his townhouse, the dagger jiggling side to side as he slammed the door. Bob walked to the main road and found Tommy. He told Tommy to take him to Thonburi Station.

Chapter Fifteen

Michael took what clothes he could find, clean or semi-clean, and pushed them into his backpack. He grabbed his passport, the small wad of cash he had left over from the night before, his Leatherman multi-tool, and a small disposable camera. He realized he had yet to get any photos of the monks, and he wanted at least one of Ramanya before he left.

Michael closed his door and began to walk to the elevator, then turned around and went back down the hallway. He knocked on Kitty Kat's door.

"Hey," she said, surprised. "What's up?" She let Michael inside.

"So I spoke to Bob today," said Michael.

"Good, I'm glad to hear it. What did he say?"

"Well, he offered to help, but we haven't figured out exactly what that will be yet. But I just wanted to let you know I'll be gone for a couple of days."

"Ok? Where?"

"I'm helping out one of the monks. Bob and I are. He's got a family situation. I think we are going to Kan-ach-a…"

"Kanchanaburi," said Kat. "It's nice there. Very interesting."

"Good," said Michael. He couldn't think of anything else to say. "Well, just wanted to let you know."

"Ok, thanks," said Kat. "Have a good trip. I think it will be good for you. To get out of the city for a while."

"Yes, I do too. Hey, we are still on for Ayuttaya next week?"

"Yes. Next week," said Kat.

"Good," said Michael. "Next week." He took a step toward the door, then spun around, and leaned toward Kat and kissed her on the lips. At first Kat snapped her head back against her wall. Michael kept his face in front of hers. Then she lunged forward, wrapping her arms around his neck, and returned the kiss, breathing hard as they both tilted their heads.

"I just wanted to say thanks for everything," said Michael.

"It's ok," whispered Kat.

Michael kissed her once more. "I'll see you when I get back."

"I look forward to it," Kat said and smiled. "Be safe."

Michael went down the hall, to the elevator, outside the building, to the corner of the street. He hailed a taxi and told the driver to take him to Thonburi Station.

Chapter Sixteen

Ramanya exited the small pharmacy that stood around the corner from his temple. Lucas, the young Thai man with blue eyes who owned it, knew and supported Ramanya and his colleagues, and whenever they needed something they could go there and get it free of charge. He also knew that Ramanya and several of the other monks traveled a few times each month to Wat Varman, an AIDS temple in Kanchanaburi that took in and tried to offer comfort and a cure to those who suffered from the disease. Lucas had told Ramanya that his own sister had died of it two years ago, so he knew how important was the work they did there. Ramanya looked in his small straw pouch and counted a dozen tablets of Codeine, some tubes of Neosporin, a bottle of Aloe, four bottles of electrolyte drink, and a couple of comic books. Again, all free of charge.

Ramanya entered the courtyard of the temple and went up to the dormitory to finish gathering his things. Tissa entered soon after, but at first Ramanya did not notice. Tissa gently grabbed Ramanya's hand, opened it, and placed a wad of money in his palm.

"You'll need it," said Tissa. "Once you cross the border. Plus, you don't have time to walk to the train station now. You need to take a taxi."

"Brother," said Ramanya. "Thank you."

They looked at each other. Two tears rolled from each of Tissa's eyes. "Whatever happens over there. Whether you find your family or the military finds you…"

"I know," said Ramanya.

"We shall never see each other again," said Tissa, his breath getting shorter and catching in his throat.

"I'm so sorry," said Ramanya.

"Our whole lives together…" said Tissa, his large shoulders shaking up and down, until at last he couldn't hold back anymore, and he placed his head in his hands and began sobbing.

Ramanya reached out and embraced him, and pressed his forehead against Tissa's. "In all of time, there has never been, nor will there ever be, a better friend and brother than you have been to me." Ramanya kissed him on the cheek, then separated himself.

Tissa wiped his eyes with the back of his hands. "I'll still be with you, wherever you go."

"Forever," said Ramanya and pressed his hands together in front of his face and bowed his head. Tissa returned the gesture.

Ramanya went down the stairs, past the children playing with the white cat, and out the red and gold gates. He found a taxi and told the driver to take him to Thonburi Station.

Chapter Seventeen

The train platform was crowded. Thonburi Station was an old railway depot on the banks of the river. Built in 1903, it was a long, open-air concrete and tin structure that for the past years only ran trains on a western-bound route. All other trains left from Hua Lamphong station, the newer, modern station in the center of the city. In keeping with the boom times, plans were already underway to convert Thonburi into a park and museum and build a new one just a few hundred feet away. But for now, dozens of vendors in their crooked stalls spread out along the edges of the platform as young backpackers from Europe and America mixed with Thai nationals, Chinese tourists, monks, and military alike.

Father Bob, holding three tickets in his hand, walked over to where Michael and Ramanya were standing. As he gave them out, he looked around the platform. On each far edge stood a pair of Thai policemen keeping watch. Nothing seemed unusual about that, but then something made him turn back to the ticket window where he had just been. Another Thai policeman now stood behind the cashier he had just purchased from. The policeman seemed to be looking directly at Bob, Michael, and Ramanya, then he picked up a phone and began speaking while still staring at Bob. After a moment, he left the booth. Nothing else happened. The two pairs of cops at the edges continued doing what they were doing. No alarms or sirens rang out. No whistles. No shouts. Probably nothing. He was probably just ordering a pizza.

"So where is *this guy* that came to you?" asked Michael.

"He said he would meet us at the border," said Ramanya. "He had other business to take care of."

The train to Kanchanaburi pulled into the station, right on time.

"Good Lord," said Michael. "How old is this train?"

Decades of caked-on grease and dirt covered the peeling paint of the old, boxy train that looked more like a subway from the 1950s. A huge crowd swelled forward, and it took them awhile to finally get on board, and indeed the inside matched the outside as rows of dull, gray, padded booths stood against peeling teal-painted walls, and rows of small fans with wire grills were nailed into the ceiling.

"No AC on this trip!" said Bob. "No sleeper cars. No first class. No second class. Very proletarian!"

Michael, Bob and Ramanya moved through the entire length of the train to the very last booth in the very last passenger car. They sat down in a pair of facing benches, Michael and Ramanya on one side, Bob on the other.

"When I took the train down to Malaysia, it was really nice," said Michael.

"Yes, I don't know why they've never upgraded this route," said Bob. "You can see it's packed every day."

"But there is a certain kind of charm to it," said Ramanya "Old style. Lucky, the trip isn't too long."

They settled in, the deckhand on the platform rang out the large silver bell, and the train to Kanchanaburi pulled away from the station. The outskirts of Bangkok stretched on for several more miles, crooked shantytowns planted on muddy roads, until at last city gave way to countryside. Michael pressed his head to the window and watched as rice paddies rolled by, their brilliant green shoots rising from shallow water; then came plantations of papaya trees, banana trees, sugarcane, and small farms of lychee trees, their plump red fruit looking like giant raspberries. Inside the train, the small fans pointing down from the ceiling did little to push away the stuffy mix of humidity and body heat that seemed to soak into the old worn walls. Vendors walked up and down the train holding large plastic buckets filled with ice, bottles of soda, and cans of beer. Other vendors strolled along with bags of peanuts, dried fruit, or chips and some sold comic books and small toys for the bored children.

A good half hour went by with neither of the three speaking. Then Michael lifted his head off the window. "You're never coming back, are you?" he asked Ramanya.

Ramanya waited a moment before answering. "No."

"So when you go back, will you still be a monk?"

"No. I will disrobe. My time as this version of myself will be over. In many ways, I will miss it."

"Could you come back to the temple if you wanted to?"

"You mean could I be a monk again? Yes. In our religion, there are no restrictions. A person may put on the robes and take them off when they wish. Although doing so too many times is not well respected. That is why now during *Khao Pansa* we have so many extra people at the temple who have decided to temporarily become a monk. It's not like Father Bob's church."

"No, it definitely is not as easy in my church," said Father Bob. "Though I've done my bit to push the limits." As soon as he said that last remark, he realized he shouldn't have done so out loud.

"What do you mean?" asked Michael.

Bob looked at Ramanya and Michael as they stared at him waiting for an explanation. He sighed and looked out the window. He could just say it was nothing. A joke. But something inside him was pushing it out on his tongue.

"Well," began Bob. "Actually I did 'disrobe' for a bit. Many years ago… I left the church for a while."

"I didn't know you could do that. What happened?"

"Um… I suppose you could say I lost my way for a bit." Again Ramanya and Michael stared at him. Bob realized the last time he had spoken of all this was to Father Timothy six years ago when he first arrived in Bangkok. "Well, in the mid-1980s, I spent some time in Beirut. Working with a Catholic relief organization in the aftermath of the Lebanese civil war. Delivering food and medical supplies." He looked at Michael. "Lebanon was a harsh place then. You're probably too young to remember all that. A lot of bad things were happening there."

"Vaguely. I was in high school. Geopolitics was not high on my radar at that time."

Bob smiled. "As well they shouldn't have been. Well… There were several kidnappings. You remember the American reporter Terry Anderson who was captured?"

"Yes, a little."

"Well… So was I."

"What?"

"Father, I'm so sorry," said Ramanya.

"February first, 1985. I was in East Beirut. Midmorning. Sunny day. I was unloading a truckload of penicillin. I never saw them. They came up behind me, pulled a burlap bag over my head, and pushed me into a car. They took me to a basement somewhere. Chained me to a wall. And left me there."

"For how long?" asked Michael.

Bob rubbed his wrists with his hands. "Sixteen months."

"Oh my God."

A silence fell over the three men and over the entire train car itself. Every other passenger was either asleep or sat silently looking out the window or a reading book.

"I never even knew why," said Bob. "They never really talked to me. They didn't beat me or torture me. They didn't make me read a statement or record a video. I often wondered if they had made a mistake. If in fact they had been looking for someone else and ended up with me instead. I was just in that room. I had about two meters' length of chain to walk around with. That was my exercise. They unchained me once a day to let me take a bath and use the toilet. Every month they gave me new pants. Every day they fed me the same thing: brown beans and rice with a spoonful of strawberry jam on the side of the plate… I had always loved strawberry jam. My whole life. With peanut butter on bread. Since I was a kid… I've never eaten it since."

"How did you get away?"

"I didn't. One day they just came in and led me outside and put me in a van. They drove me to the Syrian border. They took me out of the van, walked me to the line, and pushed me forward. It made no sense. I walked for about an hour, then a UN cargo truck came down the road and picked me up. I was flown to a hospital in Geneva. Spent a few weeks there getting my strength back and being endlessly questioned by British government, American government, CIA, I supposed. I couldn't tell them anything. There were really only two people I saw the whole time, my guards. They were young, teenagers. Just lads."

"And then you went home?" asked Ramanya.

"Yes. Eventually, I went back to England. This was now… middle 1986. I tried to get involved again, first working with another relief group at their office in London. Then I tried to get involved with a small church in the West End. But nothing felt right. I suppose I was shell-shocked. I had all the classic symptoms. I couldn't sleep.

When I did, I had nightmares. I believe today they call it Post Traumatic Stress Disorder. Most days were like swimming through a thick British fog. Anyway, by early 1987, I asked for and was granted a dispensation to leave the church, to leave my duties as a priest behind. I 'disrobed.' " Bob nodded at Ramanya. "I continued to seek treatment and went back to university to get a degree in sociology. Got involved with a city organization helping refugees integrate into British life. Worked with this wonderful family who had escaped the Khmer Rouge in Cambodia…"

Bob stopped. He was now at the part in his life that until last night he thought only two people in the world knew about: he and Sarah Goodman. It was enough. Michael and Ramanya didn't need to know about it, and he didn't want to talk about it. Time to wrap it up. "So, I was actually sort of happy for a while, but after three years, I felt the need to go back. To 'put on the robes' again. Again I asked for and received a dispensation to return, which was not easy. I had to answer many questions and write many letters. But in 1990, I did come back. Soon after, I joined Saint Thomas Ministries. Went to Kenya for three years. Then came here in 1993… And now I have the great pleasure of sitting here with you two fine young gentlemen. And I mean that most sincerely."

Michael lit a cigarette. Bob held out his two front fingers.

154

Michael passed it to him. "I didn't know you smoked."

Bob took one long, deep drag and handed it back to Michael. "I don't," he said.

"It seems we all have some pain in our past," said Ramanya.

"Most people do," said Bob, looking at Michael. "And a lot of people spend a lot of time trying to run away from it."

"In our language," said Ramanya, "we have a thing we say: wherever a man walks to, he has already been there."

Michael smirked. "We have a similar saying in my country: no matter where you go, there you are."

"Cheers to that," said Bob as he rubbed his wrists once again.

Michael sized up his two friends with even more respect than before. So Ramanya had wiped out an entire army barrack, then renounced that way of life. Bob had endured over a year of hell chained to a wall, lost his faith, wandered in the wilderness, then came back better than ever. What exactly had Michael done? Since graduating from college almost a decade ago with a near perfect GPA? Not much at all. *Squandered* is the word that now came to his mind. He had squandered everything he once had going for him. He had spent the last several years roaming the earth, looking for that burning bush to tell him what to do, finding stale bottles of booze instead.

Time to fish or cut bait indeed.

****

Another half hour rolled by, then the train suddenly began to slow down. They were in the middle of the countryside. They were not near any station. Bob looked out the window and ahead of them, far up on the curve of the track, were two Thai military jeeps. One of the four soldiers stood near the track waving for the train to stop.

"Bloody hell," Bob whispered. The image of the policeman back at the Bangkok station, staring at the three of them and picking up the phone, flipped around in Bob's mind.

"What is it?" said Michael. "Why are we slowing down?"

"Thai Military. Up on the tracks. They want to get on."

"Military? Why?"

Bob continued to stare out the window. "They might be looking for us."

"What? Why? How?"

"I saw something back at the Bangkok station. I wasn't sure... I'm on the bad side of a dirty cop in Bangkok. It has to do with the embassy siege and other things. He's trying to shake me down."

"Jesus, Bob. And you think he's tracked us down out here?"

"I don't know… I don't think Thai Intelligence service is *that* efficient. But… I don't know."

"They might just be doing a routine check," said Ramanya.

"Perhaps," said Bob as the train continued to ease down bit by bit.

Michael looked out the window, and the train pulled closer to the two jeeps. He suddenly pulled out his backpack and yanked open the top. "Well, if they are looking for us," said Michael. "They're looking for a priest, a monk, and an American drunk, right?"

"That sounds like the beginning of a horrible joke," said Bob.

"Right. And here's the punch line," Michael said and began to pull clothes out of his pack. "Time for a costume change." He took out a pair of tan cargo shorts and a light-blue T-shirt that said Karma Police in large block letters. He tossed them on Ramanya's lap. "Those are for you."

Ramanya held up the shirt. "Karma Police?"

"It's from a rock band. Radiohead. I'll explain later." Michael then pulled out a large yellow T-shirt and threw it into Bob's hands. Bob unfurled it, and it read: Never Mind the Bollocks. Here's the Sex Pistols.

"The Sex Pistols? Seriously?" said Bob.

"You're a big guy. That's my biggest shirt. We can critique

my musical tastes later." The train rolled to a complete stop. Michael pointed toward the two restrooms behind them. "Go in there and change. I'll be right back." Bob and Ramanya just stared at Michael. "Come on! Chop, chop!"

"Chop, chop?" said Bob, and then he and Ramanya stood up and each went into one of the restrooms.

Michael walked to the end of the car and to one of the vendors, an elderly man selling cold drinks from a bucket. He bought three cans of Singha beer for a total of three hundred baht. He looked out the window and saw one of the soldiers speaking to the engineer as he leaned out the control room of the first car. The other three soldiers slowly climbed out of the vehicles, each with a rifle slung over their shoulders. As Michael turned to walk back to his seat, he saw a young girl who was selling comics and toys and spied a deck of playing cards in her box. He bought it for fifty baht and headed back toward the rear of the car, keeping a close eye on the soldiers through each window he passed.

Inside the tiny bathroom, Bob looked into the small, dirt-covered mirror as he removed the white clerical collar from around his neck. He balanced it on the edge of the aluminum sink and then took off his black, short-sleeve clergy shirt. He pulled on the bright yellow T-shirt Michael gave him, surprised to find it fit him so well.

Bob scooped everything in his hands and opened the door to find Ramanya exiting the other bathroom at the same time, wearing Michael's shirt and shorts. They couldn't help but smile and shake their heads before they joined Michael back in their seats. Michael took Ramanya's orange robe and Bob's collar and shirt and stuffed them into the bottom of his backpack, piling other clothes and books on top to cover them up. He pulled out a baseball cap with a red bill, blue background, and a white letter A, and gave it to Bob.

"Here. Wear this."

"The letter A?"

"It's my baseball team. The Atlanta Braves."

"Are they any good?" asked Bob as he pulled the hat on top of his head.

"It's complicated," said Michael.

"It always is," said Bob.

Michael opened each can of beer and passed them around. He folded down a small wooden tray from a slot in the wall and took out the cards and began to shuffle.

"You guys know how to play poker?"

"No," said Ramanya.

"Just fake it," said Michael. "What are they doing out there?"

Bob looked out the window and took a sip of beer. "They are

getting on. Two soldiers in the front car. Two more in the middle car, two cars ahead of us."

"Let's play," said Michael. "And when they get here, let me speak."

"Aye, aye, captain," said Bob.

Michael dealt each one of them five cards facedown as Bob kept looking at the door to their car, waiting for the soldiers to appear. Ramanya took a sip of his beer.

Several minutes passed and then Bob said: "Ok. They are in the car next to ours. I can see through the door."

"Are they talking to people?" asked Michael.

"A few. Looks like they are checking identification."

Michael reached in his pack and took out his disposable camera and put it on the tray. The woman selling snacks came by their booth, but Ramanya waved her off. The door between the cars opened and the two soldiers entered.

"Here they come," said Bob. "One of them looks like a child."

Michael looked over his shoulder. The soldier in front indeed looked like he couldn't be older than eighteen. He barely filled out his uniform. The soldier behind him was older with sharp lines across his face, and he stopped at a young couple near the front. The young kid kept moving forward, looking from side to side at each booth with a blank, almost bored expression on his face until at last he reached their booth.

"Bonjour! Ça va?" Michael blurted out and stood up and reached to shake the young soldier's hand. The soldier pulled back in complete surprise, flustered.

"Idee," he said.

"Pardon, nous ne parlons pas Thai. Nous sommes de la France," said Michael.

"Idee!" said the soldier in a sharper voice.

"Mon ami, je regrette. Je ne peux pas comprendre ce que tout vous dites."

The soldier looked at Bob. *"Oui,"* Bob said and shrugged his shoulders. The young man then turned to Ramanya. *"Oui,"* Ramanya said and sipped his beer, shrugging his shoulders as well.

The soldier pointed at Michael's backpack sitting on the floor and snapped his fingers sharply.

"Mais, oui, oui. Surement," Michael said and gave the soldier the bag. The young military man opened it and began poking around with his finger, then started taking out each item. First Michael's socks and underwear, his Leatherman tool, and then he began to reach toward the bottom. Michael suddenly grabbed the

camera off the tray and forced it into the hand of the soldier.

"*S'il vous plaît. Pouvez-vous nous prendre en photo? S'il vous plaît.*"

The bag dropped from the soldier's hands as he fumbled with the camera and tried to push it back to Michael, shaking his head no. Michael kept pushing the camera back in his hands, then moved alongside the startled young man. He turned the camera upright in the soldier's hand and showed him where to press the button.

"*Ici! Ici! Cliquez ici. S'il vous plaît, mon ami.*"

Michael moved against the window, and Bob and Ramanya stood up and wrapped their arms around Michael, posing for the shot, all three smiling and holding their beers in front of them as if they were on spring break somewhere in Florida, until the older soldier suddenly barked orders at the young one in Thai and waved him back to the front of the car. The young soldier threw the camera on the booth and walked away. The older one kept yelling at him, and he meekly tried to defend himself, the two of them going at it as they walked out the exit door, down the folding steps, and back outside on the ground. Michael, Bob, and Ramanya watched through their window as those two met up with the other two soldiers beside their vehicles. One of the soldiers waved to the engineer to move forward, and with a couple of sharp lunges, the old train slowly began to move down the tracks once again. Bob looked the opposite way as the four soldiers grew smaller and smaller until at last they disappeared.

Michael collapsed in the booth and lit a cigarette. Bob and Ramanya took their seats as well.

"Very impressive, Master Michael," said Bob. "Very impressive indeed."

"Yes, teacher," said Ramanya. "That was very good."

"Thanks," Michael said and took a large sip of his beer. "I kind of wish he would have taken that picture."

"So you speak French?" asked Bob.

"A little. I spent some time in the Congo."

"Fascinating."

Ramanya reached over and took the cigarette from Michael's hands and took a large puff. He blew out the smoke long and slow. "Tastes good," he said.

"Ramanya!" said Michael.

Ramanya took a big sip of his beer. "Tastes good as well."

"My God," said Michael. "Take those robes off for five minutes, and look what happens to you. You're a degenerate."

Ramanya smiled and took another long drag of the cigarette. "It's been a long time," he said. "For many things," he added with a sheepish grin as a blush spread across his face.

"Oh! You cheeky bugger!" said Bob.

"Like a sailor on shore leave," said Michael, shaking his head and laughing. Bob joined him. So did Ramanya. All three laughed as the train hit full speed, pounding its way toward Kanchanaburi.

Chapter Eighteen

It was late afternoon near five p.m. when Bob, Michael, and Ramanya stepped off the train and onto the wide, spacious platform at Kanchanaburi station. The crisp country air was a welcome relief from four hours on the sticky train car, and the salty smell of fish and chili peppers frying in peanut oil swirled all around them. The walls of the station were painted a cheery yellow, and rows of large pots of flowers and ferns added more color to the pleasant scene.

"Wow. This is nice," said Michael.

"Welcome to Kanchanaburi," said Bob.

"Much different than Bangkok."

"Yes, more laid-back to be sure. There is a lot to do here, but we won't have time to do any of it! Sorry, mate. We have to walk through town to get to Wat Varman, so you'll be able to see a bit of it. But you should come back sometime. Spend a couple of days at our camp. Lots of parks and waterfalls nearby. Great hiking around here."

"Yes, I always like coming here," said Ramanya "It's nice... I need to change my clothes before we go to the temple."

"Right," Michael said and dug in his pack to pull out Ramanya's orange robes. Ramanya took them and walked toward the restroom near the ticket booth. Michael also took out Bob's white collar and black shirt and held them in his hands.

"I'm ok," said Bob, tugging at the Sex Pistols T-shirt. "It's actually very comfortable."

"And the baseball cap?"

"It keeps the sun off my face."

"Go Braves," Michael said and put Bob's clothes away.

"More importantly," said Bob as he scanned the train platform. "I'm not so easily spotted. Brilliant idea, by the way, back there on the train. You saved our hides."

"You're welcome. But what the hell is going on with this dirty cop? You think he's really tracking you? What does he have on you?"

"It's a very long story, but I know the man behind the current embassy siege. I met him several weeks ago when I was in Rangoon.

We stirred up quite a bit of trouble there. I was temporarily arrested by Myanmar police. I'm high on their naughty list. It comes down to the fact there is money to be made. Either I pay the cop or he'll collect his bounty by turning me over to the junta's goon squad."

Ramanya soon rejoined them, back in his monk's clothing, and then all three began to walk down a small side street, away from the station. Bob repeated to Ramanya what he had just told Michael.

"Yes, if the government wants you, they won't stop. Like a mad dog. Is there no way to speak to this Thai police captain?" asked Ramanya.

"Perhaps," said Bob "I had always thought he was a good egg before yesterday. When I get back, I'm hoping to try to speak to him again."

"I'm so sorry you must endure this," said Ramanya. "I'm sure it is heavy on your shoulders. It makes me appreciate even more what you are doing to help me."

"Of course," said Bob. "You know how much all of us at Saint Thomas care about you and the others at Wat Prok."

"And, teacher, you as well," said Ramanya to Michael. "I thank you so much for coming with me."

"You're welcome. I love you guys… Plus, I really had absolutely nothing else to do."

Ramanya and Michael shared a sharp chuckle. Michael reached out and squeezed Ramanya's shoulder.

The three of them turned down another street corner. Suddenly, in front of them was a long, wide field of brilliant green grass with rows and rows of identically shaped gray rectangular stones. Thousands of them. A large white stone cross rose at the far end of the field. A large marble archway stood at the entrance. Michael stopped walking.

"It's Don Rak cemetery. The POW war cemetery. From World War Two," said Bob.

Michael moved inside the archway and up to a plaque etched in the walls that read: 1939–1945 The Land on Which This Cemetery Stands is the Gift of the Thai People for the Perpetual Resting Place of the Sailors Soldiers and Airmen who are Honoured Here. He started to move into the field, then turned around to Bob and Ramanya. "Do you mind?"

"It's ok, teacher," said Ramanya. "Go ahead."

Michael came to the first row of stones. Each had a name engraved on it, and pots of flowers and plants sat beside each marker. The first stone he saw had a gold cross engraved on the plaque with a coat of arms that included a picture of a deer with large antlers. The words read: Gunner. W.T. Robinson; 3 September 1945, Age 25;

Here Lies a Lad With a Heart of Gold and Loved by All. May He Rest In Peace.

Next to that was another just like it and another and another.

"How many are here?" asked Michael.

"Almost seven thousand," said Bob.

Michael's breath caught in his throat.

"They all died working on the Death Railway. Mostly Brits, Australians, and New Zealanders. The American bodies were sent back to your country, so this doesn't even include them."

Michael continued to walk along, reading the stones. "I haven't seen one over age twenty-five." The entire cemetery was so perfectly kept and manicured, with large trees reaching out their arms to cover the fallen soldiers.

"The railway is not far from here," said Ramanya. "We'll pass it on the way to the temple."

Bob and Ramanya allowed Michael a few more moments to wander through the cemetery in silence, and then Michael nodded quietly to them that he was ready to move on. They walked along the sidewalk outside the fence and then turned onto Mae Nam Kwai Road. It was the main commercial road that ran alongside the Khwae Yai River itself and through the heart of the town. There were no skyscrapers here, only one- and two-story cinder-block buildings that contained dozens of scrappy restaurants, shops, and guesthouses catering mostly to the backpacking crowd. The road itself was a narrow two lanes that was filled with far more people walking or riding bicycles than there were cars. To Michael, it almost had the feel of a beachside town as indeed the smell of the cool air coming off the river had a slightly briny touch to it. They passed stands selling roasted ears of corn, roasted peanuts, sugarcane, fried fish on wooden sticks, as well as dozens of Internet cafés, souvenir shops, and the ubiquitous 7-Eleven stores. As they went by one bar called Checkers, which had a covered patio running alongside the street, Bob noticed the TV on the wall was tuned to BBC News, and he saw images of the Myanmar embassy in Bangkok. The three of them walked closer and stood near the entrance, catching an Asian reporter, speaking with a perfect British accent, wrapping up her report from outside the embassy walls.

"So it appears we are getting ever closer toward a resolution of this crisis. We are told that negotiators with the Thai military have received a guarantee that all hostages will soon be released unharmed, possibly as early as this evening, but most likely sometime tomorrow as details still have to be worked out regarding the transport of the rebels out of the city and back to their country. This is Janice Lee reporting from Bangkok..."

The program moved on to a story about the upcoming WTO meeting in Seattle and the protests already happening there. Bob turned to Ramanya. "Tomorrow night will definitely be your last chance. Once this is over, both militaries will move in and seal the border from both sides."

"I know. When we get to the temple, I'll try to get a message sent to Miss Sally."

The three continued down the road another half kilometer until they came to a wide circular clearing, crowded with people and ringed by brightly colored umbrellas of vendors selling food and other goods. Jutting out from the far side of the platform and crossing the river was a bridge. The bridge began with four half-circle arches, each pair facing one another, made of a latticework of iron beams, and laid upon fat cement pylons rising from the river, then a central section where the trestles ran flat, followed by five more pairs of arches on the other side. A yellow glow from the late-afternoon sun reflected off the water and covered the old structure in bright streaks of color.

Bob stopped walking and pointed. "You know what that is, don't you?" he asked Michael. "That's 'The Bridge Over the River Kwai.'"

"The one from the movie?" asked Michael. "I thought it was

destroyed at the end of the film."

"Well, yes, sort of. It's the inspiration for the story. They took some dramatic liberties, for certain. There were actually two bridges, one made of wood like in the film and this one. Both were damaged by Allied bombing, but only this one was rebuilt. This was the beginning of the Death Railway that the Japanese built during the war. You can actually go and walk across it. There is also a museum nearby, which is fascinating. Very powerful."

Michael felt a tingling sensation move from his neck to his shoulders as he thought about all the hands that raised this bridge, now lying beneath the ground in the cemetery they had just visited. He blew a deep breath out from his mouth. "Mm... I've been stuck in Bangkok so long, I tend to forget there is a whole huge country outside the city limits to explore."

"Yes," said Ramanya. "Big cities can do that to you. That's why I have always preferred smaller towns. Places like this. You feel more free."

"There really is a lot to do here," said Bob. "You can go to the Tiger Temple, the Elephant Park, the hot springs, and Wat Tham Kao Pun, which is a temple that is actually inside a cave. But not today. On to more pressing matters. Our first destination is only about a kilometer away, so as Michael so graciously said earlier:

Chop, chop!"

Michael and Ramanya smiled as they followed Bob away from the center of town.

****

The three turned down a dirt road and passed through a patch of banana trees until they came to a small open gate with book-sized tin elephants adorning each post. The name Wat Varman was written on the bronze sign in English, Thai, and Burmese, and a thin cobblestone path stretched inward to the main courtyard. A slender Thai man with large ears, wearing faded yellow overalls, was pruning a jasmine bush. Bob and Ramanya walked over to him, leaving Michael to scan the complex on his own. It was not like most temples he had seen. There were six medium-sized concrete buildings ringing the courtyard, painted half white and navy blue, with red stucco roofs. It seemed more like an old school compound, and there was only one small *viharn*, or worship house at the far end with the more usual, ornate multi-tiered roof and sharp spurs rising off each point. A few monks in the traditional saffron robes strolled outside the buildings, but beyond that it felt empty and somewhat forlorn.

The slender man quietly nodded as Ramanya continued to

speak to him. Bob took three hundred baht out of his pocket and placed it in the man's hands, then walked back over to Michael.

"So what is this place?" asked Michael.

"Wat Varman," said Bob. "From the Khmer word for *protector* or *shield*... It's a modern-day leper colony." Michael looked at Bob with blank confusion. "It's an AIDS temple," continued Bob. "Set up as a hospice to take care of those with the disease. There is another larger one in Lop Buri, northern Thailand. The monks do the best they can to comfort those who come here. Many people are dropped off by their families never to return, like leaving babies on a church step."

"That's horrible," said Michael.

"Thailand has actually been very progressive with the AIDS epidemic compared with many other countries. But there is still a lot of misinformation and shame associated with the disease, especially in the countryside. They actually have to post watchmen at the gates here at night, so if someone is dumped off, they won't spend the night on the ground. Ramanya has 'adopted' two children here and visits them a couple of times a month. He wants to see them one last time."

Michael looked at Bob's shirt. "Should you wear that here?"

Bob shook his head. "Dress code is the last thing that

concerns them here. Plus, except for the abbot, most don't know English. I should remove the hat though." Bob handed the baseball cap to Michael, who put it in his pack.

The slender man in overalls nodded to Ramanya one final time then went over to a bicycle leaning against one of the buildings. He hopped on and pedaled out the front gate. Ramanya looked over to Bob and Michael and waved them over.

"Brace yourself," said Bob, and Michael followed him.

They entered the first building into a dimly lit lobby with red-brick flooring. The first thing Michael noticed was the smell of cheap pine cleaner, like what he remembered the hallways of his elementary school smelling like after the janitors had moved through with their dirty mops. Underneath that was the smell of mosquito coils, that slightly sweet pungent odor of the cheap green spiral incense cakes that did a passable job of keeping the bugs away. He remembered that smell from his time in Africa, and then in the distance he heard a radio tuned to a classical music station, as strains of violins and harpsichord drifted through the walls. An elderly monk with silver glasses entered the lobby and bowed and greeted them. Bob introduced him as the abbot of the temple, and the abbot took Michael's hand in his warm palm, smiled, and said to him, "Welcome."

They moved inside to the first wing of the hospice, and the abbot explained to Michael each of the three main buildings was segregated into male, female, and children's sections. This was the male section, and the first bed Michael saw was a bearded man with nearly all his bones poking through his thin brown skin. The only reference point that came to Michael's mind were the photos of the wasted Jewish prisoners of the German death camps in World War Two. The man lay in a gurney with a small electric fan on the nightstand pointing at his body, which was barely covered by a red loincloth. A half-eaten orange was on a paper plate. His eyes were open but motionless as the music moved to horns and woodwinds and as flies swarmed around the bedpan beneath him; next to him was another bed, and another and another and another half skeleton, more pine cleaner and flies and empty stares and electric fans and monks standing by giving sponge baths and applying ointment to open sores. The rows of the suffering and nearly dead seemed infinite, cruelly illogical with the actual size of the building, and then they moved through to the next building, the women's ward, and yes, Michael knew this song— it was Vivaldi, *Four Seasons*—and one woman who looked no older than eighteen with a shaved head and a rainbow-colored blanket barely covering her chest looked at him and smiled. Ramanya reached out and took Michael's hand, holding it tightly, and Michael returned the gesture as his eyes glazed over and began to water, bed after bed after blank stare looking back at him.

"It's difficult, I know," said Ramanya. He pulled Michael into the next building, and this was the harshest of all. Children. Kids. In row after row. Wasting away, staring at ceilings, though some were sitting up coloring in books or playing with Legos or building blocks. Ramanya let go of Michael's hand and moved over to a pair of beds at the far wall beneath the main window. Michael walked to a nearby archway at the exit point and pressed his body against the bumpy plaster wall. French horn followed by clarinet. Bob came up next to him.

"You ok?"

"No. I've never seen anything like this."

"I would have hoped you hadn't."

Michael looked over to where Ramanya sat in between two beds, one boy and one girl. Several ants crawled over the face and neck of the boy, and Ramanya carefully picked each insect off the child's skin and placed them on the windowsill and let them scurry away to the yard outside. The boy and girl smiled at Ramanya, and Ramanya opened his pouch, taking out the comic books, drinks, and medicine he had brought from Bangkok. Light piano notes now drifted through the room.

"I have to tell you something," said Michael to Bob.

"Yes?"

"I have… some nights… I have gone to the go-go bars. Patpong Road. With the girls. Sometimes without using any protection."

Father Bob slapped Michael hard across the face.

"Ow! Fuck, Bob!"

"Are you really trying to kill yourself? To kill others? Do you see what is going on here?"

"Yes. I see it. I've been stupid. I've been careless."

"When was the last time?"

"Last night."

Bob slapped Michael again.

"Ok! Stop! I get it!"

"Go get yourself tested. Keep your willy clean for the next two weeks, then get yourself tested. There is a clinic near Wat Prok in Bangkok. It's free."

"Ok. Yes. I will. I promise."

"Let me show you something," said Bob.

He led Michael into a back room that was being used as a storage closet. Buckets and mops stood waiting in one corner of the room next to a shelf full of cleaning supplies. Another shelf had sheets and towels, but in the far corner, there was a larger steel shelf with dozens of steel trays, and each tray held rows of small white canvas bags tied at the top by twine. Labels with handwritten Thai script were attached to each bag. There were hundreds of them.

"Do you know what those are?" asked Bob. "Those are the ashes of the people who died here. Who were abandoned with no one to claim their remains."

"I—" Michael began but couldn't conjure up any other words.

"This is not something to play around with," said Bob.

Michael shut his eyes and nodded his head. He got it now as strains of a cello drifted through the air, and back into the main room the two men went, with Michael being pulled over to the window beneath where Ramanya was sitting with the two children. Ramanya was spreading antibiotic ointment on the boy's sores and motioned for Michael to sit down in the chair next to him. "This is Anong," he said, pointing to the girl. "And Prasert," he said about the boy. "They are twins, eight years old. They were born with the virus. Symptoms started appearing this year."

Michael gave the traditional Thai greeting to each and sat down next to the girl's bed. She wore a light-green smock and had a purple barrette in her hair. The boy wore pale-blue shorts and a

Pokémon T-shirt. Their lips were dry and cracked.

"What happens to them when you leave?" asked Michael.

"Pra Nanda will take over for me. He will visit them."

On the nightstand, Michael saw Thai comic books, bottles of electrolyte drink, then underneath a paper napkin, he spied a book he knew well from his childhood. He pulled out a copy of *Goodnight, Moon.*

"Do they know this book? This was one of my favorites when I was a kid."

"Yes, they like it," said Ramanya. "They don't understand all the words, but they like the pictures and the way it sounds when I read it to them."

Michael opened the book and looked at the pages he remembered his mother reading to him on a cold night while he was safe and warm under thick blankets.

"Go ahead. I'm sure they'd love to hear you speak it."

"Um… ok." He went back to the first page, cleared his throat and began to read the story.

He turned the book around to show them the pictures. The girl Anong pointed to the book and said, "Cow!"

"That's right," said Michael. "Very good." He turned to Prasert and pointed at the first page. "And this is a balloon."

"Ba-loon," repeated the boy.

"That's good, teacher," said Ramanya. "Very good."

Michael continued to read through the book, stopping on each page to point out bears and chairs and kittens and mittens and many other objects found in the timeless images. Bob came over and stood at the foot of the girl's bed, listening to Michael's voice, pitched at a low, soothing rumble. When Michael finished, Anong placed her thin hand on Michael's arm but had he not seen her do it, he would not have known it was there, so light, nearly weightless, were her limbs.

"Kăo mee duang dtaa săo," she said.

Michael turned to Ramanya for the meaning. "She said you have sad eyes."

Michael quietly nodded. "Tell her I'm working on it. I'm trying to make them happy again."

Ramanya translated to her in Thai. Michael saw a single red ant crawl across her pillow. He carefully picked it up and placed it on the windowsill where it scurried away down the outside wall.

Chapter Nineteen

The three men looked out the windows of the taxi as they went through the center of town again, then onto a road leading north into a wooded area ringed by fat, green stalks of bamboo. The ride from Wat Varman to the compound run by Saint Thomas Ministries had been completely silent as if traveling in a vacuum. A dirt driveway split off the road and led to a large stone and wood house with a wide porch surrounding it on all sides. A second long building that served as a classroom and meeting hall stood near the house with a small playground in front of it. Three guest cottages lined the woods to the rear of the yard. Bob paid the driver, and Michael and Ramanya got out and stretched their limbs. It had been a very long day, and the sun was now on its final descent.

"Hello!" Bob called out. "Any room at the inn?"

A young woman named Chrissie, with short, blonde hair,

poked her head out of the door to the classroom.

"Father Bob? What are you doin' here? I didn't know you were comin'! What a nice surprise!" she said in a lilting Scottish accent. Chrissie walked over and gave Bob a hug and kiss on the cheek. "Honey!" she hollered to the house. "Bob's here!"

Her husband, James, a tall young man with curly brown hair and a light beard walked onto the porch and waved at the group.

"What in the world are you wearin'?" she asked as she looked at Bob's shirt.

"You didn't know I was a punk rocker?"

James joined the two of them, laughing as he saw the shirt.

"Well, we always knew you were completely *off* your rocker," said Chrissie.

"Touché. It's a long story."

"You stayin' the night?" asked James.

"Yes, if you don't mind. We are heading to the border tomorrow. This is Pra Ramanya from Wat Prok. And Michael Shaw, who has been teaching there. This is James and Chrissie Harker from Glasgow. They run our camp here. They do community health outreach and run an after-school program."

James bowed his head to Ramanya and shook Michael's hand. "Ah! Our man in Bangkok. We've heard great things."

"Thanks," said Michael.

"Why are you goin' to the border?" asked Chrissie.

"I must return home," said Ramanya. "It is an issue with my family."

"Does this have to with the embassy? We've been followin' it on the radio."

"Sort of," said Bob. "Say, I'm parched. Could I get a bit of water?"

"Sure," said James. "Tonight we were just gonna eat microwave pizza and watch a movie, but now that everyone is here, let's have a proper feast! Let's see what we have in the kitchen."

As Bob and the Harkers walked toward the house, the man in the yellow overalls came riding up on his bicycle. Ramanya excused himself and went over to speak to him. Michael lit a cigarette and sat down on a circular bench in the front yard. It hadn't even been twenty-four hours since his meltdown on the streets of Bangkok, yet it seemed like weeks ago. He wondered what Kitty Kat was up to this evening and then wondered what that kiss had really been about and if it had been a smart move after all. It had felt good to be sure to have that kind of connection with someone again if only for a moment, but what kind of future could they really have when he had no idea where or in what condition he would be in next week, next month, or if the world was still standing, next year? He then thought of all the people he had left behind in the States without warning, and if he was still in any of their thoughts, or if he had evaporated, melted away like an ice crystal in the summer sun. His hands trembled a bit, and as if on cue, Bob reappeared and gave Michael a cold can of beer.

"Keep it steady, mate," he said and patted Michael on the back. Ramanya walked over to them as the man in the overalls turned his bicycle around and pedaled back toward the main road.

"Ok, Miss Sally will be expecting us tomorrow," said Ramanya. "There is still only the usual amount of soldiers at the official crossing, but she agrees with us that it won't last much longer. There are a couple of swollen creeks, now rivers created by the rainy season, in the valley beneath the refugee camp. When we get there tomorrow, I'll scout it out and find the best place to cross tomorrow night."

"Scout it out! Very good. You remembered that phrase," said Michael to Ramanya.

"Yes, teacher, thank you."

"Ok. That sounds good," said Bob.

"But there is a problem."

"Of course there is."

185

Ramanya picked up a stick and drew an outline of a road in the sand. "The Thai military checkpoint, about a kilometer before Three Pagodas Pass, is open again, manned twenty-four hours. They are stopping each vehicle and bus that travels there."

"And there's only one road in or out."

"Only one official road. There are the smuggling routes through the forest. We can take the bus to Sangkhlaburi," he said and marked the map in the sand. "Then walk into the Mon Village across the river. There is a man there who runs a bicycle repair shop. He will arrange a truck to take us to a small village next to Wat Songaria and the Huai Song Kalia stream." He placed another marker in the sand. "We can get out there, and Miss Sally will have three motorcycle drivers waiting to ferry us through, using the old logging routes through the mountains. It's a rough ride of about fourteen kilometers, but"—he drew a wide arching parallel line with his stick—"we will come out near the refugee camp. From there it's a short hike to Miss Sally's."

"But don't the authorities know about those routes?" asked Michael.

"They rarely venture in there during the rainy season. The route is usually in bad shape. But to make certain, that is what money is for. There is an entrance and an exit fee," said Ramanya.

"How much?" asked Bob.

"Ten thousand baht in. Ten thousand baht out."

"About three hundred quid each way. Ok, I can get that. There is an ATM at the bus station."

A couple of raindrops fell into the sand at their feet. "When I get home," said Ramanya, "I will send the money back to you."

"Please don't bother," said Bob. "If you find your family again, that is payment enough. Besides, what do I need money for? I'm a priest!"

Ramanya smiled. "You are very generous."

"You gentlemen plannin' world domination?" came Chrissie's voice from behind them. The raindrops began to increase in frequency as she walked up to the bench. "Looks like a storm is comin'. Let's get you inside and settled in your rooms. Then we'll start cooking."

Michael stood up. "If you need help with that, I don't mind."

"You cook?" asked Bob.

"Sure. I've always enjoyed it. It relaxes me."

"I'm finding out today you are a man of many hidden talents."

"Will you be joinin' us?" Chrissie asked Ramanya.

"Well… I am disrobing tomorrow."

"And you already broke your fast on the train," said Bob.

"This is true… Yes, I will join you. It will be my pleasure."

All four climbed onto the porch and went inside the house just as the sky cracked opened wide, sending thick sheets of rainwater rushing to the earth.

****

Ramanya held a large unripe papaya in his hands and began to peel and shred the firm green flesh. The entire group was in the kitchen of the big house, working together to prepare the evening meal. Ramanya worked alongside Michael to make *som tum*, spicy green papaya salad. As a child, he had helped his mother make it many times though the way they did was a bit different than how Michael and Thai people made it. His mother put in more curry while Thais liked it a bit sweeter and with a mix of fiery chilies.

The reality of actually seeing his mother and sister again kept rising up and drifting away. Yes and no. Belief and disbelief. Doubt continued to swirl within him as he looked around the kitchen at all these fine people he had met and come to care for. Michael and Father Bob had been so generous. Of course Tissa and Nanda and all his other brothers at the temple in Bangkok, and the sweet children Anong and Prasert as well. He didn't want to leave any of them, yet it was as if a tiger had reached into his chest and grabbed his rib cage with its claw and was pulling him toward the border. By Monday morning, he would know for certain whether his fate would be a miraculous reunion or certain death at the hands of the government. He wasn't sure if he was prepared for either of them.

Chrissie turned on the boom box on the counter, and the lush, swirling, fast tempo sounds of the pop song "Tinseltown in the Rain" by The Blue Nile filled the kitchen. "Ah! Turn that up. I love that song," said Michael.

"You like The Blue Nile?" asked James.

"Yeah, I saw them play a few years ago. Great show."

"Now, see, I knew I liked you when I met you. Anybody that likes a proper Scottish band like The Blue Nile is top shelf in my book!"

"Michael has interesting tastes in music," said Bob.

"True. I'll listen to most anything," Michael said and continued preparing his dish. He dropped three cloves of garlic into a mortar and pestle and smashed them into a fine pulp. Following that, he added four cherry tomatoes and two dried chili peppers and ground them together. A couple tablespoons of fish sauce, a whole squeezed lime, and some sugarcane water brought the mixture to a thin dressing, and Ramanya put the shredded papaya into a bowl, and

Michael poured in the liquid, and they gave it several good tosses. He then cut some long green beans in half and added them to the salad as well. Next to them, Chrissie and Father Bob were preparing *gai pad med mamuang*, stir-fry chicken and cashews, on the stove. They had marinated cut chicken pieces in soy sauce, brown sugar, and rice wine vinegar, with chopped up onions, green and red peppers, and some water chestnuts, and now poured the mixture in a hot skillet with peanut oil. Next they added two cups of whole cashews. The sweetness of the sauce and the fresh scent of the grilling peppers filled the kitchen. On the far end of the counter, next to the sink, James was making spring rolls, dipping thin rice paper wafers in a tray of hot water to soften them up, then laying them on a cutting board and filling and rolling them with boiled shrimp, thin carrot strips, mint leaves, and holy basil as well.

"Do you guys have any peanut butter?" asked Michael. "I can make a good dipping sauce."

"I do," Bob said and went to the living room to get his bag.

The music changed to the infectious hip-hop of Lauryn Hill's "Doo-Wop (That Thing)", and Chrissie turned it up louder and began to bop and move around the room. Bob handed Michael his jar of peanut butter. Michael took three good-sized spoonfuls into a large ramekin and put it in the microwave for about 45 seconds to soften it up. Then he added a few drops of sriracha sauce, black pepper, and dried garlic and stirred it all together. Ramanya laid out plates and utensils on the thick block wood dining table. Bob placed glasses and napkins while James, Chrissie, and Michael brought all the food in serving plates. Glasses of water were poured, cans of beer and bottles of grenadine soda were opened, and the dinner party settled in, ready for their meal.

"I'll say grace," said Bob. He held out his hands, and the entire table followed and linked together. James, Chrissie, and Bob closed their eyes and bowed their heads. Ramanya sat respectfully still. Michael closed one eye and kept the other open. "Dear Lord, bless this food and us to thy service. We give thanks to you for the fellowship we are experiencing tonight, and also for your eternal guidance and wisdom. We know all people are your children, and we know that you give to each and every one of us the ability to receive thy grace. For that, we forever shall strive to be thy disciples on earth. In Jesus Christ we pray. Amen."

"Amen," repeated the Harkers. Michael and Ramanya kept silent. Everyone began to eat.

"Mmm," said Chrissie. "Michael, this papaya salad is amazing. You learn to make that here?"

"No, actually, I used to make this for years, long before I

came here. When I was younger, I worked in some nice restaurants and learned a few tricks."

"And Bob said you lived in Africa as well? What were you doing there?"

It was certainly a complicated answer, so Michael took the simple route. "I was teaching."

"So my question," said Bob. "Is what *haven't* you done?"

"Oh, that's a fun game!" said Chrissie.

Michael smiled. "Yes, I've had a lot of odd experiences. Well, I've never jumped out of a plane."

"Have you ever been bitten by a snake?" asked James.

"Yes," said Michael.

"Poisonous?"

"Yes."

"Did you die?"

"No. Thankfully it just nicked me."

"How about a shark?" asked Chrissie.

"Almost."

"Been to Alaska?" asked James.

"Yes."

"Seen a ghost?"

"Yes."

"Been to the Acropolis?"

"Yes."

"Been on TV?"

"Yes."

"Ate a frog?"

"Yes."

"Had a dream come true?"

"Yes."

"Been to jail?"

One, two, three, four seconds passed as Michael pushed food around on his plate. "Yes," he said flatly.

"Oh… sorry," said Chrissie.

"It's fine," said Michael. "It's fine… Don't worry. I didn't kill anybody or anything like that… So tell me about the projects you two are doing here."

Nice pivot, thought Bob. That speed bump was quickly eased over, and the group continued their meal on a lively and upbeat note. Chrissie and James told about their health projects in the community, focusing on clean water and proper cooking and food storage techniques. Bob told a funny story about when he first came to Thailand and fell asleep on a bus and ended up in the beach town of Pattaya at four in the morning. Ramanya sang the praises of Michael as a teacher and showed off many of the new words and phrases he had learned such as *hit the ground running, top of the world, so-so,* and to go along with the current weather they were having, *raining cats and dogs.* Michael told his story about living in a house with a ghost that would sometimes wake him up at night by kicking his bed.

For dessert, they had cups of mango sorbet. Then with very full bellies and lots of groaning, they all chipped in and washed the dishes, cleaned the countertops, bopping around the room a bit more slowly to the ever-changing, booming boom box.

****

The heavy downpour leveled out to a steady rain as Michael sat down in a chair on the porch and lit a cigarette. Silent flashes of heat lightning occasionally colored the night sky and the woods surrounding the house in sheets of bluish white. Bob came out and handed Michael a new can of beer.

"Last one. You're cut off after this, ok?"

"No problem. Thanks."

"I'll join you," said Bob, opening a beer for himself and settling into the chair next to Michael. He took a couple of sips and watched the rain bounce off the front steps. "So it's time for me to hear 'The Ballad of Michael Shaw'… Why can't you go back to the

States?"

Michael took a drag on his cigarette. "Because there is probably a warrant for my arrest."

"That would do it. So what happened?"

A deep sigh rumbled out. "It's so stupid. Like I said, nothing violent. Nothing about drugs or nothing sexual. It was just a stupid thing I did. A one-time thing. I had been practically a boy scout my entire life. Never even a speeding ticket."

"So?"

Michael sipped his beer. "I had tried to start my own business."

"Doing what?"

"Film and video production. Local commercials, that kind of thing."

"Did you study that at university?"

"No. I was actually premed. I was supposed to be a doctor… I know that sounds crazy. Much of my life does. Growing up everyone kept telling me 'You should be a doctor. You should be a doctor.' So when I went to college, that's what I studied, but my heart was never in it. I had always liked doing more creative-type things, video projects, plays, that kind of thing. I actually got accepted to medical school, but at the last minute decided to go to

Africa for a teaching program instead."

"Very impulsive."

"Yes. That will be a theme in this story. So when I got back to the States, I shunned medical school again and started getting involved with film and video production. I moved to New York, to Los Angeles—"

"Ah, I can see that. A bit of Hollywood in you. Kat and Sherri certainly think so."

"Yeah. Well, I spent years working freelance on other people's projects, learning the ropes, then decided to strike out on my own. I borrowed a lot of money to try to get it started and continued to borrow more and more to keep it going. Including some from shady sources."

"You mean loan sharks?"

"Basically. It wasn't like I was slinking around in dark alleyways getting handed paper bags of cash, but it wasn't much better."

"How much?"

"To them? Twenty thousand."

"Are we talking about broken kneecaps, that kind of thing?"

"I don't know. Maybe. All told to banks and credit cards and everyone else I was in debt about five times that. I landed a few projects, but it wasn't enough. I had several projects fall through. I had an investor who was going to come on, but he turned out to be a fraud. I was looking at bankruptcy. And as if that wasn't enough, I was also married. We had been on shaky ground for a while. That started crumbling fast as well."

"Kids?"

"No… No, I would never do that. Skip out on children. But we separated. Divorce was up next. Everything was dying. Everything was crashing down on me. And then…"

"And then you really screwed the pooch."

"Yep. I took a freelance job with another company just to get some money to pay some bills, but it wasn't enough. So I forged a purchase order and had some equipment delivered to me. It was impulsive. It only took ten minutes one afternoon. I then sold the equipment and used that to make some loan payments, including the sharks. But it wasn't enough. A couple of months later, it came to light. I confessed and offered to pay back the money, but the company decided to press charges. The court date was set for a few months away… So many bad decisions and dumb moves caught up to me. I was having panic attacks every day. Waking up in the middle of the night unable to breath. I'd be driving down the street and have to fight the urge to slam my car into a telephone pole…

One Sunday I was looking in the travel section of the newspaper and I saw an airfare sale. Three hundred and fifty dollars round-trip to Madrid—"

"That's pretty good."

"Yes. Another impulse. I'd never been to Spain. I took my last credit card that I hadn't maxed out and bought the ticket. I just needed to get away for a while. Far away from everything. Clear my head. Try to figure things out. Before the court date. It was only supposed to be a two-week trip—"

"But you never went back."

"Right."

Michael took a break and sipped his beer. Bob looked out at a lightning flash and within it began to see a much clearer picture of the heavy burdens of Michael Shaw.

Ramanya walked outside. "I'm going to bed now."

"Ok," said Bob. "I'm sure you will be awake before all of us. But let's plan to leave here by 8:00 tomorrow. The first bus leaves at nine."

"Yes. And thank you again. Both of you. So much. For helping me."

"Of course. It's our pleasure."

"Sweet dreams," Ramanya said and left the porch.

Michael smiled when he heard Ramanya use the idiom he had taught him. Bob and Michael sat in silence a few moments more, then Bob looked over at Michael and raised his eyebrows to signal he was ready for more of his story.

"Right," Michael began. "So on the day I was supposed to fly back from Madrid, I was at the opposite side of the country in the town of Cádiz. It was this very dramatic, cinematic moment. I was standing on a jetty looking out at the Atlantic Ocean in front of me, knowing that America and home and all the chaos and darkness and despair of my life there was straight over the horizon. Spain, Europe, and the rest of the world were at my back, the opposite direction. And I just couldn't do it. I couldn't go there. I couldn't go home. So I took my big clump of keys for my car, my office, my house— everything, and I tossed them in the ocean."

"Yes. Very dramatic indeed."

"So I turned around and kept moving. I had no clear plan or destination at all. I just wanted to move… I picked up odd jobs as I went along. I ended up in Marbella for a few weeks, washing dishes at a restaurant run by this Irish couple. I worked as a night clerk at a hotel in Athens, Greece, for a month. Spent a few weeks as a bartender in the Greek islands as well. Ended up in Istanbul, Turkey. The day of the scheduled court date back in the States was the day I called you about this job. I was actually standing at a pay phone on the streets of Istanbul, right outside the Hagia Sophia."

"Fascinating. So because you didn't show, you assume they issued a warrant for your arrest."

"Yes."

Bob took a moment to process it all. "And how did you hear of us again?"

"From my friend Peter Marks, who works in documentaries. He was here last year working on a project about refugees in Asia."

"Ah, yes. I remember him now. Wonderful chap."

"He told me about the projects you guys ran, and I had written down your name and contact info just in case."

"Well, you had perfect timing. The day you called was the day after the previous teacher just found out his mother had taken gravely ill and had to return home to England."

"Yes. I was surprised when you agreed. So I spent the last bit of my money on a one-way plane ticket from Istanbul to Bangkok. When I stepped off the plane, I had about sixty dollars to my name."

Bob shook his head. "Mm… Well, that is quite a story to be sure."

"You guys should probably do a better job of screening people in the future."

"No! Not at all. Don't think of it that way. I'm very glad you made your way to us. I have no regrets whatsoever."

"Thanks."

"I care much less about what a person has done in the past, and more about what they do today and tomorrow. That is the important thing. Besides, as you said, you didn't do anything heinous. We have all done foolish things. Couldn't a good barrister take care of it for you?"

"You mean a lawyer? Maybe. But since I blew the court off once already, I doubt they'd be so forgiving."

"So you think if you go back you will get more jail time?"

"Probably…"

"That is a sticky wicket to be sure."

"You know, before I came here, I had visions that I would be living in a Buddhist temple, deep in the woods somewhere. As a monk as well, sitting on the floor, meditating, looking for enlightenment… Instead, I found more beer and Patpong Road."

"Well, you *chose* to find that. Don't forget that."

"I know."

"I certainly believe there are some events in a person's life that God has a direct hand in creating, but that he gave us free will for the rest of it… Speaking of Patpong, I hope today at Wat Varman scared you straight?"

"Yes. Yes, it did. Most definitely."

"You will get tested?"

"Yes, I will. I promise."

"Good."

Chrissie then walked onto the porch waving a video cassette in her hand. "Hey, we're gonna watch a movie. We've got a new one from the States. Called *The Matrix*. About computers takin' over the world. We thought it was fitting with Y2K on the way," she said, laughing.

"That sounds great," said Michael. "We'll be in in a minute."

"Ok. We've got popcorn too!" she said and went back inside.

Bob turned his chair around to face Michael directly. "So I have to ask you something, but I don't want you to think I'm pouncing on you in a moment of weakness. But are you religious at all?"

"Not really. I mean, I'm not an atheist. I believe in the *possibility* of God or some other force. Went to church most every Sunday growing up. I was raised Episcopalian."

"Ah, yes. Catholic-lite. All the ceremony, half the guilt."

Michael smiled at that. "I guess I've been mostly self-absorbed these past years. Haven't thought a lot about it."

"Well, that is precisely my point. Now I want you to understand something first. I, and everyone else at Saint Thomas Ministries, we are not missionaries in the classic sense of roaming the earth trying to convert the heathens of the world. We don't do that. We don't proselytize. Our mission is focused on humanitarian activities. We have been involved with Ramanya and the monks at Wat Prok for several years now, and never once have we tried to convert anyone. We have respect for all faiths. But... What I'm trying to get across to you is that I fiercely believe a person needs some kind of spirituality in their lives. They need to be able to look to something outside themselves. Whether it be Christianity, Buddhism, Hinduism, Pantheism—whatever. It's a personal choice, but if one doesn't have that outlet, life can be such a massive weight that one person can't carry it all by themselves. You have to have some way to lighten the load. Otherwise, it will crush you. It will kill your spirit, which is I'm afraid what has been happening to you."

Michael watched a burst of wind blow the rain in a swirling angle. "I think you are right," he said quietly. He dipped his finger in a puddle on the railing, then used the water to extinguish his cigarette. "You know, when I left nine months ago, I didn't tell anyone. No one had any idea where I was going. And this entire time I've been gone, I've had no contact at all with anyone back home.

They have no idea where I am. They probably think I'm dead."

"I'm sure there are some people who would like to see you come back from the grave."

"Mm…"

Bob watched Michael run everything over in his head. "It's a lot to think about, I know. At the risk of harboring an international fugitive, if you decide to stay here, I'll help you out like we spoke about. You are welcome to continue working at the temple. If not, I can help you that way as well."

"Thanks… You're a great person."

"Well, I don't know if I'd go that far. I'm definitely very good." Bob and Michael shared a quick laugh. Bob put his hand on Michael's shoulder. "You know you said you had hoped to spend every day sitting cross-legged in the woods, looking for enlightenment. Well, maybe all this time you have been receiving enlightenment, just in a way you never expected."

"Maybe."

"Smashing. Let's go watch a movie about computers run amok."

"Sounds good."

They left the porch and went inside the house.

Chapter Twenty

As Ramanya slept, he had a dream he was walking through a forest. He was wearing sneakers and shorts but no shirt, and he had a machete in his hand as he hacked away at the thick bushes and trees blocking his path. He heard someone whistling behind him, but every time he turned around, no one was there. Eventually, he came to a clearing in the forest, and there was a small pond in front of him. In the middle of the pond were two children, a young boy and a young girl, riding up and down on a seesaw. Each time they went down, their feet dipped into the shallow water, and each time they went up they shouted and laughed. He turned to his left and saw along the banks of the pond a large pile of sticks and twigs set up in a triangle, rising several meters off the ground. Suddenly, it burst into flames, crackling and snapping as the wood burned, and thick black smoke swirled up in the sky. He looked back to the pond, and the children were gone, but the empty seesaw continued to rise up and down, dipping into the water each time. Then a white cat appeared at his feet and dug its claws into his shorts and pulled itself onto his shoulder. It perched in the bend of his neck and purred and hummed as the fire roared higher into the sky, and Ramanya could feel the heat on his skin until at last a woman's voice rang out behind him. Before he could turn around, she simply said: "Hello there."

Part Three

Sunday, October 3, 1999

Jonny notices a ray of light creep farther into the lobby as the sun crawls over the horizon. Everyone on the floor still sleeps. They have blankets and pillows or cushions from chairs or sofas. His men are resting as well, their rifles leaning unattended against the walls. Jonny watches them as he has all night.

From outside, from beyond the embassy walls, the trucks and tanks from the Thai military are silent too. Only car horns from the normal rush of early morning traffic can be heard along the large thoroughfares surrounding this street. He watches a red and gold spider spinning a web in the bushes outside in the courtyard, the silk strands sparkling in the light. A man behind him clears his throat and rolls over onto his side, eyes still closed.

Soon it is all going to be over, and soon I can go home. We have made our statement. We have shown who we are and what we can do. I like this country. I want our country to me more like here. More smiles. No one smiles at home. I want to make people smile. I want to—

He sighs out and rubs his hands across his eyes. He looks at the piles of broken glass swept in the corner.

Is this what I really want? I've spent most my life with a gun in my hand. I'd gladly trade it for a shovel or hoe and a plot of land. Maybe it is time for others to carry this forward.

He looks once more at the pile of bodies lying peacefully on the floor.

No one has been seriously hurt. Just a few cuts and scrapes. No one has died. No one has to. I will make certain of it.

The phone at the front desk rings. One of the soldiers stirs awake and looks at Jonny. Jonny nods his head and the soldier answers the phone.

Jonny watches the spider continue to climb around the bushes outside.

I am so very tired today.
Maybe I just need to sleep…
But not yet.

Chapter Twenty-One

When Father Bob woke at nearly 6 a.m., everything felt different. The new day felt different. Everything felt lighter and freer than it had in a very long time. Maybe it was because he had had the best, deepest sleep in months, or maybe the molecules of the air itself, scrubbed clean by the heavy rain, had separated somewhat, eased off one another, dialed down the electricity of their chemical bonds and allowed the atmosphere in this part of the earth to relax and expand and to *breathe.*

He lay in bed looking through the holes in the mosquito netting that tumbled down from the ceiling. On the nightstand was his prayer book. He loosened the net from the corners of his mattress and let it snap free and clump together in a single long pile. He picked up the book and rolled over on his back in the bed and opened it to a passage marked for travel:

"O Almighty and merciful God, who has commissioned Thy angels to guide and protect us, command them to be our assiduous companions for our journey until our return; to clothe us with their invisible protection; to keep from us all danger of collision, of fire, of explosion, of fall and bruises, and finally, having preserved us from all evil, and especially from sin, to guide us to our heavenly home. Through Jesus Christ, our Lord. Amen."

He planned to say that with Michael and Ramanya later in the morning before they left this compound and took the first step on today's journey. As he closed the book, the photo of the young lad Gabriel fell from where he had placed it in between the back cover. It was the first and only picture he had ever seen of his son. He had Sarah Goodman's hazel eyes to be certain, as well as her freckled cheeks. Bob had known her since they were both that age, growing up in Watford, England, and he remembered the purple lunch pail she used to carry to primary school, and the butterfly shaped barrettes she used to wear in her hair. He recalled often running into her on weekends at the playground in Cassiobury Park, as well as sharing the stage with her during many holiday festivals, and they remained friends and classmates, but nothing more than that, all the way through their teenage years at St. Michael's High School. Then Bob went off to Cambridge, and she followed her parents to London, who by that time had begun to rise high in the banking world. It was not until nearly a year after Bob had left the church, first weekend of May 1988 to be more precise, when he had been shopping in a Sainsbury's supermarket in the Mayfair district in London, in the cereal aisle, that he saw her again. It was nothing preposterous, such as lost love at first sight; there was no sudden swelling of violins when they met and began talking. Just a few moments to recognize each other and then a quick hug and peck on the cheek as he took a box of Frosted Flakes and she Shredded Wheat. She looked fit and healthy, slender with her light-blonde hair in a ponytail, wearing a blue sundress and sandals. They exchanged numbers, but weeks went by before Bob finally called to meet her for lunch near where she worked as an assistant manager at the Dorchester Hotel. They grabbed a couple of sandwiches and bags of crisps from a corner shop and walked across the street to Hyde Park. They sat down on a bench near the Serpentine and had their meal, watched the swans flutter about in the pond water, and swapped stories. She told him about her leaving university to get married and how that quickly failed after three years because of her ex's constant philandering; her time spent working at resorts along the French Riviera, starting as a desk clerk, then moving her way up in other leadership posts, which eventually brought her back here to London. He told her about his time at seminary, his work overseas, and then all about what happened in Beirut, his return, his decision to leave the church, and his current studies at King's College London. She said she remembered hearing some of that in the news when she was in France but didn't realize it was him, and as tears welled up in her eyes, she gave Bob a long hug and said she was thankful he had made it back alive.

Their relationship was a slow burn. A couple of months went by, and they met for dinner at a curry shop. Then several more weeks after that, they met for a round of tennis. Bit by bit, however, the time in between seeing each other and being apart grew shorter and shorter. One evening, early fall in '89, Bob was invited to a party at a flat of one of his classmates. Sarah agreed to go along, and it turned into quite the bohemian affair as the group of twenty or so sat on the floor drinking wine, listening to music, a rock group called The Stone Roses, he remembered, and for the first time, Bob smoked pot. As Sarah passed the joint to him, she said, "There is nothing in the Ten Commandments about not smoking a dried-up weed." Soon after Bob inhaled, he felt the deepest sense of calm and enjoyment since he had returned home to England, and it was something of a revelation—those secular pursuits he had missed out on all these years. At the end of the party, Sarah invited Bob to come over to her place the following week, and when he arrived at her small townhome on Wesley Street near Marleybone she cooked seafood pasta, salad, and garlic bread. After dinner they opened a second bottle of wine and shared a joint, and then they kissed for the first time. Sitting on the floor. Leaning against her sofa. A light rain splashing against her windowpane.

"That didn't feel weird," she said as she brushed her fingers against her lips.

"Well, thank you. I guess," said Bob.

"No, I mean it felt right. It felt natural. We've known each other so long, I wasn't sure." She leaned in again and they kissed longer and deeper. "Have you ever kissed a girl before?"

"Why? Am I mucking it up?"

"No, not at all. I was just curious since, you know, you became a priest."

"I didn't become a priest until I was twenty-four. I was quite the swinger up until then."

"Really?"

"No. Of course not. I did have a passionate minute or two in high school with Jenny Crow. Behind the arcade."

Sarah punched Bob in the arm. "Jenny Crow! She was horrid. She had one eyebrow."

"Ah, yes, she could have used some tweezers, to be sure. But at that point, beggars couldn't be choosers."

Sarah poured more wine, then pressed her shoulder into Bob's side, and Bob wrapped his long arms around her and held her for a very long time.

A few weeks later, Friday the thirteenth, October 1989, Bob remembered, they returned from seeing *Miss Saigon* at the West End. Bob walked Sarah to the stoop of her building. He reached down and gave her a kiss, and then she pressed her fingers to the back of his neck, moving up into his thick blond hair, and whispered in his ear: "I want you to come in tonight, and I don't want you to leave."

It felt right, it felt natural, it felt like the most perfect thing in the world, and it continued to do so for several more weeks—until it didn't anymore.

An unseasonably warm evening in mid-December, they lay in bed with her ceiling fan gently swirling above them. Sarah had both hands wrapped around Bob's head and ran her fingers through his hair. They had barely spoken the entire night, and in fact, the previous few times together had been characterized by an awkward sputtering, like a wall of vines that had slowly been growing between

215

them.

She kissed the top of his head. "Do you miss your old life?"

"I'm not sure. It seems so long ago… Why do you ask?"

"I saw the brochure. From Saint Thomas Ministries. It fell out of your satchel."

"Oh, that. I saw that in a clinic I visited. It seemed interesting."

She continued to rub her hands over his head. "They have a lot of programs. Kenya, Botswana, Cambodia, Thailand… It's what you used to do, isn't it?"

"Well, yes. But I can do that with other groups. I'm doing that here in local communities."

"But is this what you really want to do?"

"That's quite a large question… What do you want to do?"

She smiled. "I asked you first."

Bob slowly sat up in bed. "I have to be honest. Yes, lately, all this, this life has begun to feel a bit strange."

"How so?"

"It's… It's as if I have been shown a glimpse of an alternative life. A *what if.* Like Scrooge or Jimmy Stewart. The first year after I returned was a blur. I was a zombie. But then, after seeing you, little by little I stepped into a new world. And at first it was fun. It was thrilling. It was all so new. But…"

"But you are getting tired of it?"

"Not that. It's more like sometimes I feel like I'm standing beside myself watching another version of myself. It's odd… What about you?"

"Oh, I always feel like I'm watching another version of myself. Nothing has ever really felt like a perfect match for me. You have been the closest thing. But…"

"But?"

"But, I'm sorry, darling, no. It still doesn't feel like a perfect fit."

"Does anything ever feel like that?"

"Maybe it's an illusion. But before what happened to you in Beirut, did you ever feel detached? Did you ever feel like you were not doing what you were supposed to do?"

Bob sat for several moments, thinking back to the first time he traveled overseas, stepping off the plane onto the tarmac in Ethiopia in 1975 when he was just twenty-six. "No. I never felt like that. It always felt right. I never questioned anything."

"Could you go back?"

"To the church? After all this?"

"Who would know?" she said. Bob raised his eyebrows.

Sarah pointed her eyes to the sky. "Besides *Him*, of course. You haven't committed any sin. Really."

"That certainly depends on how you look at it… But, what exactly are you saying? Should we stop seeing each other?"

"Darling, do you really see us getting married? Changing nappies? You punching a clock?"

"I do care for you. Deeply."

She pressed her palm against his face. "As do I. Which is exactly why I am saying this."

The holidays were soon coming, and Sarah had plans to spend them with her parents, so they decided to take time to do a bit of pondering. It would be the last time they ever saw each other. On Christmas Eve, Bob went to midnight mass, sitting in the pews in street clothes, then came back to his flat to see a gold foil envelope pushed under his door. He opened it to find a folded map of the world. At the top, he saw written in Sarah's handwriting: Looks like a perfect fit. New Year's came and passed, and still, he had not heard any word from Sarah. He rang her several times, went by her home, but she was never there. Finally, near the end of January, he went to the Dorchester Hotel hoping to see her.

"Sarah Goodman?" repeated the concierge on duty. "She resigned a few weeks ago."

"Where did she go?"

"I have no idea. It was rather abrupt. Left us in a bit of a lurch." He walked to the front desk and asked two of the clerks, but they didn't know what had happened to Sarah either. Bob stood in the lobby for several moments, then began to walk out the front door when a middle-aged woman in a manager's uniform ran up behind him. "Are you Bob?" she asked. "Bob Hanlan?"

"Yes."

She handed Bob a small beige postal box. "Sarah left it for you."

Bob took it and walked across the street to Hyde Park, to the Serpentine and to the bench where they had sat on their first lunch meeting. In the box was a small mini-cassette recorder. He pressed play, and Sarah's voice drifted through the air. "My dearest Bob," she began. She was pregnant. She had known when they last saw each other. She had been thinking hard the past few weeks about perfect fits and plans and parallel lives, and she had decided hers was not to be in London, not to be with him, because he needed to return to his true life as well. She would move to a smaller town, to a simpler life. She would raise the child herself, on her own. Her parents had plenty of money, so Bob need not worry about that, but she asked only one thing of Bob: that he was to never see her or the child. It would be better that way, for her, for the child, and better for Bob as well. It would be their secret, and no one else ever needed to know. She cared so much for him, but she was certain this was for the best. She had put a postcard in the box, a tourist photo of Hyde Park, and she was sure he was sitting there now, at the Serpentine, listening to this. The card was addressed to a private box she had set up for them and only them to communicate. They could use this over the coming years. If he agreed, please reply and send it along.

Bob watched the swans paddle and dip their heads in and out of the water. He took out a pen and wrote one single word on the card: "Yes." He walked to the street and dropped it in the first mailbox he saw.

Once a year over the past nine years, he had received a letter from her, usually near the holidays. She always told Bob everything was fine, but she never sent photos. Three times Bob had sent her a small care package of children's clothes, books, and toys, the last time being Christmas of last year. Maybe that was how Manny had found her, he now wondered. Or he could have easily tracked down former classmates who would have remembered Bob and the striking blonde woman. But how had he known for certain the child was his, without sneaking into his room the middle of the night and taking swabs of DNA? Then it hit him that Manny hadn't known. Not for sure. It had been a bluff, and Bob's reaction when he saw the photo had given Manny all the proof he needed. The final piece he needed for his blackmail puzzle. Bob had played right into his trap.

****

Ramanya and Michael met each other in the kitchen for breakfast at 7:15 a.m. and decided to cook a simple meal for the whole house. They boiled a dozen eggs, peeled and chopped up half a dozen mangoes into cubes, and toasted and buttered fourteen pieces of bread. They found jars of orange marmalade and strawberry jam in the fridge and set them on the table. They put on a large kettle for tea and set out glasses of cold water as well.

Bob entered wearing his black clergy pants, but only a plain white undershirt up top. "Morning, gents."

"Still in street clothes?" asked Michael.

"More practical." He looked at Ramanya. "We are getting you home today."

"Yes. I believe so."

"You seem to be in a very focused mood," remarked Michael.

Bob poured hot water in a teacup and sat at the table. "Good night's sleep does wonders. Pass the toast please." Ramanya handed Bob the plate of bread. "And the jam," said Bob.

Ramanya and Michael looked at each other. "It's strawberry," said Michael.

"Yes, I know," said Bob. "Please pass it here." Bob took the jar and spread a good amount on two slices of toast. He took a large bite, chewed it vigorously, and swallowed it. "Scrumptious," he said. "It's been too long."

James and Chrissie entered and went directly to the radio sitting on the countertop. "You should hear this," said James as he adjusted the dial.

A reporter speaking with a British accent crackled to life. "And to repeat, we can see the hostages now beginning to leave the embassy. They are... walking in a single-file line, arms raised. Walking calmly toward the front gate, where they are being met by Thai military officers. They are being directed to a staging tent on the corner of the street where medical personnel are checking them for any injuries. It appears all are in good physical shape up to this point. Then they are being put onto a bus parked next to two military trucks. Again, the hostages are leaving the embassy, but the armed Karen rebels are still inside, and negotiations are still happening about how they plan to be extracted..."

"We're on the first bus this morning," said Bob.

"We'd drive you there ourselves, but our truck is in the

garage. Won't be ready till end of the week," said James.

Chrissie looked at Ramanya. "You're hoppin' the border tonight, aren't you?"

"Yes. I can't go through the checkpoint. I'm wanted by the military. It's a complicated story."

"We don't need to know. Is someone there to help you?"

"We've made arrangements, yes," said Bob.

"I'll ring downtown and get a taxi sent here for you," said James.

"Let me make some sandwiches for you to take on your trip," said Chrissie.

"Thank you. You are so kind," said Ramanya, and then he and Michael began to clear the table and wash dishes.

"So I guess you won't be goin' to church today?" Chrissie said to Bob.

Bob smiled. "Not today."

Once the kitchen was clean, Michael went back to his guest room to brush his teeth, wash his face and hands, and finish packing his bag. Ramanya walked outside and ducked into the empty classroom building and sat down on the floor for a quick meditation. Bob continued listening to the radio, but no more details were released. At 8:00, everyone met in the front yard as a taxi pulled to a stop. Chrissie gave each of them a bag of sandwiches and dried fruit, and a hug.

James shook their hands. "Good luck to you," he said to Ramanya. He turned to Bob and Michael. "Feel free to stop here again on your way back."

"Of course. We will see you on Monday," said Bob as he, Michael, and Ramanya settled into the car. They waved one last time as the taxi pulled away, moving past the long wall of bamboo trees and back out onto the paved road, heading toward the center of town. "Hope everyone is well rested. It's going to be a very long day. And night."

Chapter Twenty-Two

The bus station in the center of town was quickly filling up as the three men got out of the taxi. Each of the two dozen terminals surrounding the large concrete and tin shelter had a bus idling within it, heading to various tourist destinations such as Hindad Hot Springs or Erawan Falls. Bob gave Michael some cash.

"Go ahead and buy the tickets to Sangkhlaburi," said Bob. "There is an ATM across the street. I'll go there and get the rest of the money we need."

He crossed the parking lot and passed a row of vendors selling banana shakes, roasted vegetables with chili paste, and steamed dumplings. The green and red logo of Thai Farmers Bank on an awning waved in the early morning breeze. It stood in the middle of a string of shops and restaurants, and Bob went to the outside ATM machine and took out four withdrawals, two each from his checking and savings. Next to the bank was the bright-blue sign of a Siam Travel shop. They were ubiquitous in Bangkok, popping up on every other street corner, selling packaged tours to Pattaya, Phuket, Angkor Wat, and dozens of other attractions. Bob looked over his shoulder, back at the bus platform, then opened the glass door of the travel agency, and went inside. As he stood at the counter waiting to be called, his back turned away from the front entrance, a pair of shadows rose up and shimmered in the reflection of the store window, those shadows that for the past few weeks Bob had been seeing out the corner of his eye, those slithering phantoms he had been certain were lurking around streets and alleyways, marking down his every movement. They were now real. They had arrived, and they planted their boot-covered feet on the outside sidewalk and waited for him to exit the store.

As soon as Bob saw them, their leather cloaks over khaki pants, he recognized them as the two men he had seen several weeks earlier, standing at the end of his alley, smoking cigarettes and staring at his house. The tallest one, with short-cropped salt-and-pepper hair, grabbed Bob by the arm and without speaking led him around to the back of the building, away from the parking lot and out of sight from most everyone else. The other man, shorter and with crooked teeth, took out a slender, bright-green piece of plastic with a small antenna. Over the past year, these mobile phones had exploded on the streets of Bangkok. Teenagers were now going crazy over them, able to buy cheap, brightly colored phones in almost every mall and shopping district. Crooked Teeth gave the phone to Bob. Bob turned it from side to side, not sure which was the right end and what to do with it. Big Guy pressed it to the side of Bob's face.

"Are you trying to leave us?" Bob heard Manny's voice say on the other end.

"My, this thing is remarkable," Bob said. "I feel like I'm in the same room with you. It *was* an interrogation room last time, wasn't it?"

"I'm glad you are so impressed."

"Bloody hell, Manny. I'm not running away. I'm in the middle of helping someone. I'll be back in the city tomorrow. We can talk then."

"Did you contact the Goodmans?"

"No! I haven't had time. There has been a lot going on."

"Yes, especially your friend Jonny and his group at the embassy."

Bob clenched his jaw, felt his neck begin to tighten up. He looked at Big Guy and Crooked Teeth who stood on either side of him. Bob was still pretty fast, but if he tried to run, they would probably catch him. And run where? Best to play along with Manny. Try to buy more time.

"Look, when I get back tomorrow, I'll come to your office and we can discuss it."

"That won't be necessary. You can give me your answer now."

Bob felt his cheeks burn and turn red. He couldn't speak.

"If you don't pay me," Manny continued, "my friends from the other side will. It's that simple... It's just business."

Bob sighed out. How had this happened? He remembered the note Father Timothy had written him when he had gotten out from the Burmese jail: Stupid move. He could hear Timothy telling him: "Next time, you're on your own." He could see Sarah's face, the last time they had been together, that warm December night nearly ten years ago. He could smell the stale cigarette and cinnamon of Manny's breath as he leaned over him the last time they had met at the police station.

He saw himself running, constantly running, looking over his shoulder for the rest of his life.

Bob looked once more into the blank, stupid faces of the men in front of him. He'd had enough.

"Ok, Manny, here's my answer," Bob said, speaking slowly

and enunciating each word. "You can kiss my white, British, Catholic arse."

Bob pushed the phone back into Crooked Teeth's hands. Bob stood with his tall, slender body pressed against the cinder-block wall, his breathing spiraling faster and deeper, and the sharp pain in his shoulders and neck now screaming so much as to nearly turn him blind.

****

The clock on the bus platform read 8:57, as the driver of the 9:00 to Sangkhlaburi blew a whistle announcing they were almost ready to leave.

"Where the frick is Bob?" Michael asked and strained his neck to look over the crowd of people stretched out in front of him. "He's been gone forever."

"There he is," said Ramanya, pointing the opposite direction. Father Bob walked slowly across the backside of the station, his head down.

"What is he doing?" Michael motioned to the driver that the last of their party was almost here. When Bob reached the open door to the bus, he took his ticket from Michael, handed it to the driver, and climbed on board without saying a word. Michael and Ramanya looked at each other then followed him onto the bus, walking the length of the aisle to a pair of seats near the back. Michael looked down at Bob as he put his bag on the overhead rack. "You ok?"

Bob briefly looked at Michael. "Fine. Thanks, mate. Just feel a bit woozy, that's all."

"You look a bit pale."

"I'm sure it will pass."

Michael took his seat next to Ramanya as the bus began to back away. Bob sat by himself and squeezed the back of his neck with his hands. He then dug into his pack, took out his jar of peanut butter and a plastic spoon, and jammed it in, cramming a large blob in his mouth. As the city streets began to thin out and turn into a two-lane highway, Bob realized he had forgotten his plan to say that travel prayer this morning with Michael and Ramanya by his side.

****

They seemed to have the road to themselves, rolling, rolling through the countryside, moving deeper into the wilderness, as any remnants of city or town life disappeared. Cinder-block and tin buildings gave way to huts made of bamboo walls and thatched roofs, and the bus stopped at seemingly empty points along the highway to let out a dusty traveler or two who would fade away into a wall of trees. The road climbed higher and higher into the densely forested hills of Khao Laem National Park, moving by places with exotic names such as Hellfire Pass. Past and present melted together in the minds of each of the men, memories swirling around them like the streaks of green flying by in the windows. The cave where Ramanya and Tissa lived for several weeks after the burning of their village as the bus passed by a thin waterfall spilling from a rocky cliff. The gray eyes of Michael's wife the last time he saw her, hardened and unforgiving, before she turned around and walked down the brick steps of their house, the bus turning a sharp curve to reveal a rope bridge sagging over a ravine, connecting two crooked hilltops. Bob standing tall in a boxing ring at age nineteen, pounding down Sebastian Moore, his slow-footed classmate at Cambridge, as the bus made a descent into a mist filled valley, white clouds clinging to the forest walls like cotton candy soup.

Seconds to minutes to hours rolled by and just before noon the bus arrived in the small town of Sangkhlaburi. As they stepped out onto a dirt street in front of the bus stop, it seemed to Michael to be not much more than a large village. The air was thick with the smell of diesel fuel and burning wood, and even all the nearby sounds seemed muted and muffled as if one had a pillow to one's ear. No building rose over one story, and people moved along the roads as if they existed in a closed glass globe, ignorant and uninterested in outside visitors.

"We have to cross the bridge into Mon Village," said Ramanya, pointing across the hazy blue horizon. "Our next contact lives over there."

Michael and Bob followed him down several dusty streets until they reached the riverbank and the sprawling, striking bridge known as Mon Bridge, or Saphon Mon, as Ramanya told them, a ramshackle wooden structure that looked like it was made from one million tangled matchsticks. Floating bamboo houses swayed back and forth in the water as the three men climbed upon the planks of the bridge and moved forward to the smoky hillside on the other end; the smell of burning charcoal grew stronger the closer they got to the village named Wang Kha, founded fifty years earlier, Ramanya explained, when an abbot from the Mon tribe named Utama marched sixty families out of the Tenasserim Hills, past the refugee camps along the Burmese border to this little peninsula at the meeting point of river and lake. Aided by the generous indifference of the local Thai population, they created their own parallel homeland.

As Michael stepped off the bridge, a group of women walked past them wearing the traditional Mon costume of long white blouses and flowing red dresses, holding bright-red parasols in their hands.

Ramanya led them down a dirt road populated by packs of chickens, and then Wat Wang Wiwekaram suddenly rose in front of them, a towering gold pagoda with two majestic statues of giant white lions standing out front, each rising ten meters tall, adorned with jeweled headpieces, mouths open and eyes trained toward the clouds, guarding the entrance to the temple.

They came to a shack with wheels, handlebars, and other bicycle parts hanging on the bamboo walls. Ramanya knocked on the open doorway, and a gray-haired man with wire-rimmed glasses emerged. After exchanging greetings, the man dug into a mud-stained cooler and handed each of them cold bottles of water, then waved down an alleyway to a shirtless young boy. He and Ramanya spoke in their native Mon language for several minutes, and then all four sat in silence, slowly sipping on the water. A small breeze spun one of the wheels dangling from the tin roof of the shack, like a quiet wind chime.

Michael looked back the way they had come and saw several people walking in a single-file line toward where they sat. The people were of all ages: children, teenagers, middle-aged men and women. A teen boy led the procession and played a small bamboo flute, ringing out sharp, lilting notes while behind him a teen girl held what appeared to be a carved wooden semicircle, lined on the inside with rows of small brass cymbals, like an inverted tambourine. She struck the instrument against her leg with each second step, adding a shimmering backbeat to accompany the flute. The parade squeezed into the narrow alley. Each of the people approached Ramanya, bowed their heads, and placed various gifts on the scratched wooden table before him. Many left pieces of candy known as *jaggery*—light-brown rock candy made from toddy palm trees and rolled in coconut flakes or tamarind dust. Others placed a single red flower before him. Ramanya greeted each person and the mumbled words *"Dangoon, dangoon"* rolled off the people's lips.

Michael turned to Bob. "What's going on? What are they saying?" he whispered.

At first, Bob seemed to ignore Michael and did not answer, until Michael rolled his eyes and threw open his hands in frustration.

Finally, Bob said, "They are coming to thank him. For all he did back home. Fighting the government. Trying to protect their way of life."

Michael watched the ever-growing pile of gifts. "Our boy's a rock star. He's a folk hero!"

"Mm," Bob grunted.

For nearly twenty minutes, the line of those coming to pay respects to Ramanya continued. As it began to come to an end,

Ramanya gave Bob and Michael each a piece of the *jaggery*. Michael put it in his mouth where it quickly began to dissolve, the tart and sweet flavors covering his cheek and tongue, causing him to purse his lips. Ramanya then gathered the rest of the candy in a cloth and gave it to Michael to put in his pack.

A small pickup truck with peeling green paint pulled up in front of them. "*Dangoon, dangoon,*" Ramanya repeated, thanking the owner of the shop, as Michael and Bob climbed in the back. The crowd of people split in half, and the truck slowly rolled down the dusty corridor. Ramanya stood up in the back of the truck and gave one final *wai* to the people of the village, pressing his hands to his face and closing his eyes.

****

The truck jerked down a back road out of the village, drove over a short concrete bridge around the outskirts of Sangkhlaburi, turned down a bumpy dirt path that cut through a sugarcane field, then reconnected with the main highway. The loose ends of Ramanya's orange robes flapped like flags in the rushing wind. The choppy air massaged Michael's face, and then he looked at Bob sitting silently in the corner of the truck, and Bob's eyes seemed almost sunken.

After several bends in the road, they came to a stop on the

other side of a small bridge above a swollen stream known as Huai Song Kalia. A one-room roadside restaurant stood on the western side, with a pair of goats nosing in the muddy courtyard. A girl of about eight or nine sat at a small crooked table on the eastern side where she was selling bars of soap, cigarettes, and cans of evaporated milk. The driver motioned to the three men that this was where they were to get out, and before he pulled away, Bob took a one hundred baht note from his pocket and gave it to him as a tip.

"This is it?" asked Michael. "There is nothing here."

"Precisely," said Bob.

"He speaks!" said Michael. "We had begun to think someone had snipped out your tongue."

Bob smirked as the truck quickly spun around and took off the way it came, leaving him to connect eyes with the young girl and her pile of unwrapped soap. Without speaking, she pointed up the narrow dirt path behind her. The three walked along the path for about twenty meters, rising up a small hill until several bright flashes pulsed from behind a clump of papaya trees.

"There," said Ramanya, pointing to his left. "That's our ride."

They moved off the path toward the trees and came across three slender Thai men in their early twenties sitting on Honda dirt bikes next to a boulder that marked the beginning of an old logging trail. Ramanya briefly spoke to each of them in Thai, gathering their names.

"Nattapong," Ramanya said, introducing driver number one. The young man wore cut-off red shorts and a yellow tank top and carried a machete in a shoulder strap. In his hand was the signaling mirror, and he grinned and flashed it a couple of more times in Michael's eyes.

"Hey, enough," Michael said. Nattapong continued to grin.

"This is David," Ramanya said, pointing to driver number two. He had a thin mustache and wore rolled-up khakis, a large backpack, and a tattered blue baseball cap with the cartoon character Tweety Bird embroidered on the front. David held out his hand and took ten thousand baht from Bob, put it in a plastic zip-up sandwich bag, and stuffed it in his backpack as Bob climbed on the bike.

"And this is Teerapat," Ramanya said, motioning to driver number three. He had a thick black beard, mirrored sunglasses, and a pistol in a holster on his hip.

"I'll take the badass with the gun," Michael said and climbed on the back of Teerapat's bike. "Helmets?" Michael motioned to him, pantomiming with his hands. Teerapat smiled and shook his head no. "How long will this be?" Michael asked Ramanya.

Ramanya climbed onto the back of Nattapong's bike.

"Depends on the conditions of the roads. If we are lucky, only an hour or two."

"That's being lucky?"

"Bpai gan tùh!" shouted Teerapat and each of the three motorcycles spun their back wheels in the dirt, lurching forward, swaying back and forth before catching the proper balance and then shooting off into the wide, thick forest.

Chapter Twenty-Three

Twenty minutes was all it took before the forest path sunk into a melted pond of heavy, red mud. David's front wheel had been nearly swallowed whole.

"Well, that's just beautiful," said Michael.

As each of the men took turns trying to free the cycle, the wet earth grabbed hold of their ankles and calves, making it harder and harder to move. Nattapong scaled a teak tree in front of the mud hole, and Teerapat dug inside the backpack and took out a coil of rope. They tied it to the front wheel of the cycle, then tossed it up to Nattapong, where he created a pulley, pressing his feet into a large branch and bracing his back against the trunk. Bob and Michael and Ramanya pushed the bike from behind while the other two drivers pulled the wheel from the front. Several false starts, several backtracks, then finally the cycle flipped on its side, where it was easier to drag it forward and out of the mud. For the other two bikes, the men made an assembly line through the center of the tree line off to the side of the sunken path. They lifted the bikes above their heads and passed them over to each person, the last person in line running forward to take the front of the line, repeating this over and again, twisting and turning the cycles to squeeze sideways in between narrow trunk space, until finally all three bikes lay on a dry patch of ground. The six men collapsed to the floor of the forest. David and Bob took out bottles of water from their packs and passed them around.

"That was fun," said Michael, his chest heaving up and down.

"I don't think we've even gone two klicks," said Bob, wiping sweat from his forehead.

David adjusted his Tweety Bird cap, pointed toward the sky, and shimmied his fingers downward, indicating rain. "Big water," he said. "Big problem."

Michael pointed at his cap. "You like Tweety Bird?"

David smiled. "Tweety Bird, yes! Pooty-tat!"

Nattapong and Teerapat began to scrape off the thick mud from the front wheels and frame of the rescued bike, using sticks they found lying on the ground. As they worked, they spoke quickly to each other in Thai, then looked over their shoulder at Ramanya, pointing to their wrists.

"They want to know what time we need to arrive," said Ramanya, "I told them before nightfall."

"Well, that's only about seven hours more," said Michael. "I take it this is not the express route."

"No," said Bob. "It's not."

David stood up and raised the cycle straight up, got on the seat and tried several times to start the engine, but each time it sputtered out before catching fire. Michael sighed. He opened his pack and took out his Leatherman multi-tool. "It's the fuel line," he said. "There's probably dirt in it. I can fix it."

"Of course you can," said Bob.

"I used to have a bike like this."

"Of course you did. You know, the more time I spend around you, the more impressed I become."

"I take that as a compliment?"

"Yes. You should."

Michael didn't even waste the energy needed to stand up but rather rolled over and over on his side until he was next to the cycle. He lay on his back and used his tool to pry off the plastic engine casing, then dug into the dozen screws holding the carburetor and gaskets in place, and pulled out the plastic fuel line. A red clump of clay sat in the middle of the tube. He wrapped his lips around the gasoline-laced opening and blew hard several times until the mud flew out into the air. Next he dug deeper into each cylinder to scrape out grit and mud residue there as well.

As Michael continued to work on the cycle, Ramanya looked up toward the canopy of the forest, and his eyes stopped at the bend of a thick branch of a Chinese cedar tree about five meters above them. His breath skipped a beat, and he placed his hand on Bob's shoulder and pointed to the tree. Bob grew still a moment, then placed his hand on Nattapong's shoulder, who placed his hand on Teerapat's shoulder, who then tapped David on the back. David grinned, then placed his hand on Michael's back, interrupting his work on the bike. Michael sat upright, followed David's pointed finger, and saw the great spotted cat, stretched out along the tree limb, its long tail swaying slowly back and forth, its head perfectly still and calm, looking down on all six of the men.

"Is that... a leopard?" asked Michael.

"Yes," said Bob. "It's magnificent, isn't it?"

"It's very rare," said Ramanya.

"It has probably been watching us the whole time," said Bob.

David stood up and pretended to pull back a bow and let an invisible arrow hurl toward the cat. Michael pulled at his pants leg, bringing him back down. "No," he whispered. "Don't get it mad at us."

Exquisite stillness, except for its slowly curling tail, its wide eyes motionless, the leopard's yellow and black spots only slightly blended in with the brown bark and shadows. Bob looked straight into the great cat's eyes and felt the stiffness in his own shoulders and neck loosen and melt away. A thin shaft of sunlight then broke through the treetops and formed a white oval on the ground near his feet. Bob closed his eyes, leaned in, and turned his face into the light, feeling a disc of warmth cover his brow and the bridge of his nose. A powerful sense of calmness filled his body and mind. He took several deep breaths, felt a smile growing inside him, and stood up to stretch his heavy limbs.

Michael sat on the bike, slammed down the kick starter over and over until it finally growled to life. He immediately looked up at the leopard, but again the cat was nonplussed, continuing to sit motionless and calm, giving no judgment nor twitch of involvement.

They were free to move forward and continue on.

****

They hit a long stretch of dry but very bumpy trail as the cycles climbed higher and higher into the mountain range. Sharp jolts hit Michael's spine and neck as Teerapat jumped up and down over each exposed root or rock sticking out of the worn path. The air grew a bit colder as the altitude rose and thinned out, a refreshing change from the usual web like humidity of the jungle.

The forest opened up into a small clearing, and rising from the center of the field was a large stone sculpture, grayish black from years of harsh weather, a four-armed deity with the body of a man but the head of an elephant. In one hand, it held a rope in the shape of a noose and in another a spiked shaft. It sat cross-legged on top of a giant rat, which held a large acorn in its paws. Swirling letters of Thai script were carved into the base of the statue, putting forward a long-lost proclamation. The monster was a singularity and seemed orphaned and out of place, but at the same time to Michael it appeared to be guarding a secret, an invisible, even sinister gateway into another world. It was one of the strangest things he had ever seen. It was carved in stone, yet it felt alive as it looked down on the travelers and challenged them to come forth. Each of the three drivers did just that, pulling their cycles into the field and stopping in the shadow of its body.

Michael climbed off the bike as David took a red blanket out from his pack and spread it on the ground. "We're having a picnic? Here? In front of this?"

Nattapong spoke to Ramanya as he spread out small plastic

containers of food. "He says it's good luck to have a meal here."

Michael looked at the elephant head's eyes, following him like an old portrait in a haunted house. "Doesn't look very lucky to me. What is it?"

"A disciple of Luang Pu built it many years ago," said Bob. "There is a large sculpture garden on the other side of the country on the northeast border with Laos called Wat Khaek, built by a man called Luang Pu, a Brahminical mystic who had these visions of Hindu-Buddhist deities. He created dozens of creatures like this. It's a pretty amazing place. Very spooky though."

"One of his disciples came here to start another version. He only completed this one statue, then disappeared. No one knows what happened to him," said Ramanya.

"Yes. Very lucky indeed," said Michael.

Teerapat motioned for them to sit down. Michael took out the bags of sandwiches Chrissie had made for them and passed them to Bob and Ramanya: chicken, avocado, and tomato on Vietnamese *bánh mì* rolls. The drivers dipped their fingers in a small bowl of stewed vegetables and then pinched off small balls of sticky rice and popped those in their mouths, and David pulled out a half-empty half-liter bottle of Johnnie Walker Red Label Whisky from his pack. He poured a small shot inside the screw-top cap and offered it to

Michael. Michael looked over at Bob who quietly nodded his head and held up one finger. David then passed the cap to all the others in the group as they each, including Ramanya, took one single shot of the whisky. From within the forest, the sharp whistles and whoops of an unseen family of gibbons echoed around them, adding an extra layer of surreal flavoring to their most exotic of picnics.

Michael and Ramanya joined the drivers in a post meal cigarette.

"Are you excited? Nervous?" Michael asked Ramanya.

"Yes. Both."

"And you trust this man who found you? The one who came to you in Bangkok?"

"Yes. It is hard to describe, but besides just him, there had been other signs, other feelings speaking to me."

"You're going to miss Tissa. I know you guys are close."

"Yes. That was the hardest thing. To say goodbye to him. You will continue working with the others at the temple?"

Michael hesitated. "Yes."

"But you are not sure for how long?"

"No."

"This is not your home here. I understand that. Perhaps it will soon be time for you to rejoin your family?"

"Perhaps."

"I'll miss you too, teacher," said Ramanya. "It is a wonderful thing you have done coming here to help us."

"Well, I had many different motivations driving me here. Not just charity."

"It doesn't matter. What matters is what you have done. And it has been a good thing. Everyone else at our temple has felt the same way."

"Thank you. That means a lot." Michael took a final drag of his cigarette. "How will we know if you made it there safely? If you found your family?"

Ramanya looked Michael in the eyes. "You will know."

It took a moment for Michael to understand what he meant, and Michael nodded his head. "I hope you are right." He reached out and placed his hand on Ramanya's shoulder.

Father Bob stood up. "Ok, we need to keep moving. Let's pack up and hit the road. Chop, chop!" he said, clapping his hands.

Michael and Ramanya looked at each other and grinned. "Father Bob is back," Ramanya whispered.

"Yes, he is," said Michael. "And just in time."

The group packed up their items, then climbed back on the cycles, leaving the statue to wait for another group of travelers.

Nattapong signaled they had eight kilometers left to go.

****

They entered a thicker and much darker section of the forest. The trees here grew larger and wider as they moved up the mountain. Multi-legged giant krabak trees with sometimes as many as half a dozen thick, stone-like fins jutting out from the massive base of their trunks began to crowd out the rest of the vegetation. In some places the path all but disappeared, leaving them to twist and lurch the motorcycles forward as best they could over the jagged forest floor.

Then, the image the group least wanted to see appeared before them: they came across one of the fallen giant trees, completely blocking their path.

"So much for the good-luck picnic," said Michael.

They parked the cycles. The girth of the trunk lying on its side now turned to a height of more than two meters. The length of the great tree stretched beyond their sight in each direction. Nattapong and Teerapat went opposite ways into the forest looking for another path around while Michael placed his hand on the tree. It was rough and hard like concrete but with no branches or cuts or outcroppings they could use to climb over it, much less pull the three motorcycles. David took the machete and gave several sharp whacks into the trunk, making a few shallow nicks in the wood. Even if they had a chainsaw, it probably wouldn't do any good.

The other two drivers soon came back from the woods with their legs up to their knees covered in black mud. Nattapong shook his head side to side. "No go," he said. "Boom boom."

"Boom boom?" Michael asked.

David dug into his backpack and took out a tin canister labeled Nestlé Quick cocoa powder and three empty cans of Carnation evaporated milk.

"We're making chocolate milk?"

They looked inside the opened tin and saw a container of fine, dark-black granules. "It's black powder," said Bob. "Blasting powder. These guys work as part-time loggers as well."

"So we're going to blow up the tree?"

"That appears to be the plan."

"Under other circumstances I'd say that would be pretty cool. These guys know what they are doing?" Michael asked Ramanya.

"I can help them," said Ramanya. "This used to be my job."

Nattapong motioned to Bob and Michael to move the cycles farther back on the path. Ramanya and the two other drivers went to the tree and used their hands to dig out three indentations in the soil underneath the trunk, each about a meter apart. Next, they each took one of the empty milk cans and carefully poured the black powder from the Nestlé tin. They filled each can about three-quarters full then placed them in the freshly dug holes. Michael watched David take a pack of sparklers, the cheap kind kids used on the Fourth of July, and stick one in each of the cans, then take a roll of black electrical tape and cover the cans, wrapping the sparklers in place upright. Ramanya poured a thin trail of black powder along the ground, connecting each of the cans. Each man took a box of matches. Michael and the others hid behind the cycles, about twenty meters from the tree as Ramanya held up his hands to make sure his two partners were ready. He nodded, and each struck a match, pressing the flame to the sparklers, which burst to life in white and blue crackling light. They ran fast, ducking behind the row of motorcycles as the first, then the second, then the third explosion shook the ground, sending dirt, smoke, and shattered wood high into the forest canopy. The six men covered their heads as rocks and shards of the tree trunk rained down upon them.

The tree was battered but not beaten. Much of the bottom half of the trunk was shredded, but the top half, except for two large cracks, was still intact.

Ramanya walked forward to examine it. "It's not enough. We have to do it again. We need a total break to be able to have any chance of pushing or rolling even a small section out of the way." Sticking his feet into the new gashes, Ramanya was able to climb on top, wrapping his orange robes above his knees and tying them off to give him more room to work. David followed him up on the trunk, catching the machete Nattapong tossed up to him and began hacking away at the largest crack until they had a gash boring into the center of the tree.

"So now what?" asked Michael.

"We have to pour the rest of the powder into the tree, try to blow it out from inside," said Ramanya. "Do you have your lighter?"

Michael dug in his pocket and took out his orange plastic cigarette lighter. "Yes."

"We need to use that as an ignition. The sparkler won't work. We won't have time to get away."

"Ok, MacGyver," said Michael, then realized that no one else there would have any idea what he just meant. He tossed the lighter up to Ramanya. David hacked away a small groove and poured in some of the powder. Ramanya set the lighter on top, then poured a short trail to the hole they had bored in the trunk. He emptied the rest of the tin can into the hole.

"Is that it?" asked Bob.

"Yes. That is the last of the powder."

"I still don't understand how you are going to ignite it," said Michael.

Teerapat pulled his pistol out of his holster. He smiled beneath his mirrored sunglasses.

"This, I gotta see."

Ramanya and David climbed down off the tree, and the group, except Teerapat, took cover behind the cycles. Teerapat stood straight, raised the gun, and took aim at the orange plastic cylinder sitting in the gash of the trunk. His first shot missed, about five centimeters to the left, sending a splinter of wood flying into the bushes.

"Tux making," said David. "Keep steady."

Second shot and the tree exploded from within, sending sharp missiles flying toward the group as Teerapat quickly spun around and dove to the ground, and the cycles teetered over, crashing into the dirt. Michael rolled over a few times dodging the wooden spikes falling from the sky. When the ground finished shaking and the last of the debris tumbled to earth, the group stood up and saw a large section of the tree now almost completely gone and separated into two. Ramanya helped Teerapat to his feet and patted him on the back. A big smile broke out over Teerapat's face. He raised the gun to his lips and blew across the barrel, took a bow, then put it back in his holster. "Cowboy," he said and pretended to adjust a hat on his head.

They still had some work to do, using the machete and their hands to smash up and clear away the rest of the exploded wood, but after about twenty minutes, they had a path wide enough to roll each of the cycles through. Once on the other side, the six men stood still and tried to get their heavy breaths down to a normal rate.

"How much further do we have?" asked Michael.

Nattapong held up one hand, all five fingers spread wide.

They climbed on the bikes, ready to ride away. "Five klicks," said Michael. "Well, it can't be worse than these were."

****

All that was left of the small footbridge was one single plank of wood. The old wood sagged and stretched across the gap in the road, about five meters in length. Beneath them, what used to be a narrow creek was now a river swollen and engorged by months of rain. It rushed downhill with a frothy roar. Large boulders poked out of the rapid water, splitting the stream into different paths.

"You've got to be kidding me," said Michael as the group of six looked at their latest hurdle.

They were three kilometers away from their final destination.

They had been traveling for three hours. They were covered in dirt and sweat. Their shoulders and backs slumped, and their legs felt like they were made of concrete.

A thick swarm of blue-and-yellow-winged dragonflies rose up and spread out over the stream, fluttering in their faces, lighting on their arms and hands. Nattapong took off his shoes and stepped onto the black, slimy wood board that felt like stepping on a wet bar of soap. He motioned to David to scoop up dry dirt and spread it along the beam, hoping to add a bit more friction and surface area to help them pass without falling. David handed Nattapong his backpack as Nattapong continued to edge along, his bare toes curling over the wood. Ramanya followed him, pushing the motorbike forward. They grasped the front wheel and back wheel tightly as if it were a balance bar used by a tightrope walker. Within ten minutes, they had made it across to the other side. Next were Teerapat and Michael.

"Short steps!" shouted Bob. "Move slow."

Michael took off his shoes, placing them in his backpack, and grabbed the front wheel of the cycle as he stepped onto the wood. He wobbled back and forth a few times then caught his balance as Teerapat steadied the back of the bike and pushed it forward. Ramanya and Nattapong stood at the other end ready to help them over. "Don't look down," said Ramanya. "Just look at me, teacher." Halfway across, the plank sagged and began to shimmy, twisting the front wheel back and forth, causing Michael to drop to one knee to keep from tumbling over into the water below. He pressed his fingers into the wet wood, closed his eyes, and took several deep breaths, then stood up and continued forward. His eyes locked onto Ramanya's eyes, moving step by step, closer, closer, until his front foot reached out and touched dirt on the other side. Ramanya grabbed Michael's shoulder and pulled the rest of his body onto land as Nattapong jerked the bike forward. Teerapat gave it a final push, leaping the final gap and tumbling to the ground as the cloud of dragonflies danced all around them.

Bob moved out in front with David pushing the cycle from behind. Smooth, smooth, little by little they moved across until Bob could just about stretch his leg to the other side... Then wings and legs suddenly scratched David's eyes and face as several of the dragonflies flew straight at his head. As he tried to swat them away, he lost his balance and fell to the water below, the back wheel of the bike skidding off the beam, nearly pulling Bob down with him. Bob grabbed the front handlebars fiercely as Ramanya and Teerapat lunged forward on the plank to help him. Together the three of them pulled the bike forward and onto the ground, then all five ran along the riverbank.

The rushing water pulled David along and slammed him up against one of the large boulders. He screamed out, his head just above the water, his body pinned against the rock. Nattapong quickly took the coil of rope from David's pack and tied it to the tree nearest the bank. They formed a line along the rope with Teerapat in front followed by Michael. Ramanya and Bob anchored the rear. Teerapat and Michael descended into the cold, rushing water, their arms coiled tightly around the rope for support, their feet frantically grasping for solid surfaces, until they reached where David's head kept fighting to stay above the rapids.

"Good, good," Teerapat shouted. "We here."

He reached out and grabbed David's shirt, and Michael moved to the other side. They wrapped the rope around his chest just beneath his shoulders, and Teerapat struggled to tie a knot in the water spraying all around him.

"Move?" asked Michael. "Can you move?"

David shook his head no, then spoke to Teerapat in Thai. "Leg," he translated to Michael. "He say leg no good."

Michael dove his head beneath the stream and opened his eyes. In the swirling muddy water, he was just able to see a rock pinching David's left leg. He came up for air, then went down again, wrapping one arm around the rope for balance, and with his free arm, he pushed the small boulder back and forth until it loosened and flew away with the undercurrent. From above him, he could hear David scream out in pain, the sound slicing through the roaring water. Michael came to the surface and helped Teerapat lift David and lay his body on top of the stream as Ramanya, Nattapong, and Bob pulled the rope from the riverbank. They jerked and twisted David's body as he writhed and shouted until at last they pulled him up on land. Next they helped Teerapat climb out of the water, and as Michael was ready to get out, he saw David's Tweety Bird cap stuck on a twig poking out from the shore. He grabbed it and then rolled onto the ground.

They could see the broken bone sticking out from the skin, just below David's left knee. Nattapong took off his yellow tank top, ripped it in half, and wrapped the shreds tightly around David's limb, the bone snapping and cracking as he screamed. Trying to calm him down, Teerapat held David's head in his hands, and David mumbled over and over in Thai.

"He's saying truck, truck?" asked Bob.

Ramanya translated. "He wants to stay here and wait for them to return with a truck."

"Fine. As soon as we get to town, I'll pay for someone to

come get him. I'll pay for all his treatment as well," said Bob. "We'll take care of him."

Ramanya translated back to David and gave him a sip of whisky from the bottle. The other drivers spread the red blanket on the ground, then asked for Michael's multi-tool. They punched holes at each end of the cloth, sliced the rope in half, tossed one-half of the rope to Michael, and then both sides threaded it through the holes. Next, three men carefully lifted David and placed him in the center of the blanket as Michael and Nattapong pulled the rope around two nearby tree trunks, lifting it and David off the ground in a makeshift hammock. They tied off the ends of the rope around the trees.

Rapid and shallow, David's breathing sputtered. The other two drivers placed their palms on his forehead and held his hand, trying to ease him down. They spoke in low voices and David quietly nodded his head. Michael came up next to the hammock, and gave David his wet cap; David's watery eyes, seared by pain, looked back at him.

"Hang in there, buddy," Michael said, knowing David wouldn't understand his words, but hoping his voice and the look on his face would communicate what he wanted to stay.

"We can get to town within twenty minutes," said Bob. "As long as there are no more problems."

"I'll drive his bike," said Michael.

The engines cranked to life, blue smoke poured from the exhaust pipes, and David in his hammock grew smaller and smaller, the cycles rising up the mountains. Moving and spinning, bumping and jolting forward, dry paths cutting through the dark forest, they kept driving, driving, one kilometer past, then two, then three, until at last the trees began to thin out and disappear. One house, then another, then a small paved road appeared before them. From the top of the hill where they came to a stop, they could see down the road to the center of town. They had finally made it to Three Pagodas Pass.

Chapter Twenty-Four

It was just past 5:00 p.m. when they pulled up to Café Sugar, the last restaurant in a short four-block arch of tin-roofed stores and shops that made up the "town" of Three Pagodas Pass. It stood directly across from the three pagodas themselves: three smallish triangular spires, each only about three meters high, made of limestone painted white and wrapped in green and gold cloth, standing in a circular field. The camel hump double peaks of the Tenasserim Hills rose in the sky behind the monuments, and in front of each pagoda was a small shrine where people left flowers or other offerings. Though quaint to look at, Michael thought, they certainly didn't live up the exotic sound of their name. They looked like large playing pieces from a child's board game, stuck in grass, decorated with garlands.

The group parked their bikes and peeled themselves off the

seats, each of their bodies feeling like they had been worn down to painfully aching nubs. The first thing Father Bob did was to give Nattapong the final ten thousand they owed him for completing the journey. Then Bob half hurried, half limped over to the lone ATM near the open-air tourist market. He emptied out as much of the money from all his accounts as he could, pulling all the cash that was left from inside that plastic and metal machine.

The group then walked onto the patio of the clean, bright café where about half a dozen tourists lounged on benches covered by blue and white checkered tablecloths. A teenage boy wearing a tan waiter's outfit knew immediately who they were and went into the kitchen. A middle-aged Thai woman soon emerged, walking with perfect posture and precise movements. She had her thick hair in a ponytail, wore a thin layer of makeup, a strand of pearls around her neck, a perfectly crisp, clean, white cotton Oxford shirt and green trousers. Michael thought she was rather attractive in a polished, professional, confident way—like a successful lawyer or politician. She looked at the group, covered in dirt and sweat, and motioned for the waiter to prepare a table.

"We had some problems," said Bob.

"So I see," she said in a formal British accent.

"Hello, Miss Sally. It is very good to see you."

She had a strict face broken apart by warm, light-brown eyes. "Where's David?"

Nattapong explained everything to her, and then she motioned for them to sit down at a bench that had been set with bottles of cold water, skewered chicken on bamboo sticks, and spring rolls.

"Eat a quick snack. You all look famished. Then we get moving. We have a lot to do. I'll get a truck ready to get David." She moved quickly but without nervousness to the edge of the patio and signaled to a vendor on the sidewalk selling mangoes. He came over, and she whispered in his ear, and he took off down the roundabout, past the three pagodas.

Nattapong took the stack of cash Bob had just given him and the other pile from David's backpack and gave them to Miss Sally, who in turn gave them to the waiter and instructed him where to put it. "You probably haven't heard the latest," she said and sat down to join them. "But the Thai military has agreed to bring the rebels. Here. Tonight. They are going to fly them up in a helicopter and drop them off. The leaders across the border are furious. The Myanmar military will be here by morning. In full force. We have to go tonight…"

As they dug into the food and water, they could look across

the road to the border crossing, the red and white gates and demarcations indicating the end of Thailand and beginning of Burma, the same line Bob had been pushed across only a few weeks ago. Only two soldiers could be seen, standing around, at this moment, without any urgency.

"Somebody was asking for you," Miss Sally said to Ramanya.

"Did he have a scar on his chin?"

"Yes."

"He is the man who came to me in Bangkok. He will go with me tonight."

"I'll get a message to him. You all will stay at my private boarding house up on the hill. But when this happens late tonight, I won't be there. I will be at home with my daughter. I have enough trouble with the junta as is without them thinking I'm involved with this. It has become very expensive doing what I do."

"If you need more money, let me know," said Bob. "I'll leave some for David's treatment as well. Here…" Bob reached in his pocket and pulled out another twenty thousand baht stack of bills, fresh from the machine.

"Thank you. You are very kind." She turned to Ramanya. "Your best bet is the valley below the refugee camp. The creek there is very full, and it is at a good angle, away from the checkpoint. You should wait tonight for the helicopter to come. That will be the perfect distraction. Everyone in town and at the border will be focused on that."

A red pickup truck pulled in front of the café. They each finished their last bite of food and stood up. Bob said: "Ok, Michael use one of the bikes and go with Ramanya to scout out the crossing point. I'll go with them to get David and take him to the clinic. There is a small one a couple of klicks down the road. He'll be able to at least get some morphine. We'll meet back at the boarding house. You know where that is?" Ramanya nodded yes. Bob put his hand on Ramanya's shoulder. "You ready for this, mate?"

"Yes."

"We're on the home stretch."

Ramanya looked at Michael. "I'll explain later," said Michael.

Miss Sally motioned to the waiter. He reached behind the door to the kitchen, then tossed a can of fluorescent spray paint to Miss Sally who caught it with one hand and gave it to Michael. "Make sure to mark your path on the way back," she said.

"Right," Michael said and put it in his backpack.

"All right," said Bob. "Let's go then."

****

A few raindrops fell from the sky as Michael, with Ramanya sitting behind him, drove the motorcycle up a hill. The paved road gave way to a red-dirt path that brought them to the crooked wooden gates marking the entrance to Halockhani Refugee Camp. Beyond the gates, the path cut along a jagged line of mud huts with thatched roofs on one side and a wall of trees on the other. The ground behind the trees sloped downward, moving into a thickly forested valley, and on the other side of the valley, through breaks in the trees, they could see the hills that rolled inward to Burma. They could hear, but not see, the movement of the swollen water far below.

Michael and Ramanya entered the camp on foot. The light from the fading afternoon was much dimmer here, and it took a moment for their eyes to adjust. Flat, nearly lifeless faces, perched atop thin bodies barely covered in dusty clothes peered out from the huts, from around wooden poles, turning around from tables and benches as they moved along the path now getting dotted with rain. There was an overall lack of motion in the camp—adults, children, even the animals seemed to barely move, as if there was nowhere worth moving to, which is why the actions Michael and Ramanya created—walking without hesitation, certain, purposeful, and focused—seemed to provide some form of entertainment to the residents, like a TV show come to life.

Near the last row of huts, they entered the tree line and began their descent. The sound of the raindrops got a bit louder as they bounced off the tree canopy above them, but very few of them actually made their way to the ground. There was only a very small footpath that was hard to follow as it snaked its way in and out of the tangled brush, and they passed a couple of small mud huts that had been built in the forest, as spillover from the refugee camp and for people wanting more privacy. A small cooking fire smoldered in the doorway of one of the huts, but no one could be seen nearby. The woods sloped downward at a fairly steep clip, then gave way to several large boulders jutting out from the earth. Ramanya and Michael climbed over one of the large rocks and dropped down into a narrow passageway that ran between the stone walls, leading down to the riverbank.

The dark, reddish-brown water moved at a good pace, but it was nothing too intimidating. The distance across the water was about thirty meters, and on the other side, a large tree branch with three forks, like a crooked trident, stuck out from the bank and poked the air over the water. Behind it, the dark-green coastline stood as a silent, thick curtain covering the country from the rest of the world, a country of rich history, of impoverished people, and of bloodstained streets.

"That's home," said Michael.

"Yes," said Ramanya. Ramanya looked down the bank toward his left, craning his neck outward to see just a tiny speck of the official gates at the border crossing. He could just see the roof of the guardhouse. "This should be a good spot. During the day, if they happened to be looking, the guards might be able to spot someone swimming across. But at night, especially tonight, with all that will be going on, we should be able to make it. Though sometimes they hire locals to comb through the woods at night to try and catch people."

"How far do you have to go once you get there?"

"The man said my family are in a small mountain village about twenty-five kilometers away. We can be there by first light."

"And once you find them, then what? Won't the military still be looking for you?"

"Yes, they always will, but they have blind spots. There are places up in the hills they rarely go. We could build something there."

"And you won't bring them here?"

"You saw the refugee camp up there," said Ramanya, motioning with his head to the top of the valley. "That is no place to live. Even the Mon Village we were in earlier today, it's not the same thing as being home. Truly home. Where you belong."

Michael nodded. He took out the can of paint and shook it. He sprayed a swath of bright yellow on a nearby branch. Then the two of them retraced their steps and every twenty meters or so, Michael sprayed a rock or tree. The raindrops caused a few small paint streaks to drip downward, but most of it held up and dried quickly. As they climbed up the final large boulder, the rain at that spot fell unimpeded from the sky, covering the rock in a slick glaze. Just as he reached the top, Michael's left foot slipped out from beneath him, and he fell to the passageway below, his left arm scraping a sharp angle in the rock. A deep gash began to bleed heavily, and he writhed on the dirt floor. Ramanya jumped back down next to him. He dug in Michael's pack, took out his multi-tool, and slashed off a ribbon of fabric from the bottom of his orange robe. He wrapped it tightly around Michael's wound.

"Thanks," said Michael.

"Are you ok to walk?"

"Yes, yes. It hurts like a motherfucker—sorry—but let's go."

"I'm sure Miss Sally has some medicine and supplies at her

place."

Ramanya took Michael's pack and helped to pull him up over the large boulder. They went up the slope to the top of the valley. When they passed the small forest hut, a young girl now tended to the cooking fire, roasting two ears of corn on a pan made from an old rusted hubcap.

****

David's skin was bluish white, and Bob piled on oil-stained burlap bags and blankets on top of his body to keep him warm. He was only semiconscious as another yellow dragonfly landed on his face. Bob gently swatted it away. Teerapat and Nattapong lifted the hammock from the ground underneath the trees, and put David in the back of the pickup truck.

The truck moved as quickly as it could away from the swollen creek and back up the mountain. Bob placed his lower leg next to David's head to keep it from banging against the metal side of the truck bed as the craggy road jolted them all from side to side. As they neared the top of the mountain, Bob took a deep breath in, sucking in the fresh forest air that smelled like a just-opened bag of white sugar. Thailand was definitely his favorite. Out of all the countries he had lived in and visited, sixty-four at last count, this place once known as Siam, this nation known as "The Land of Smiles," the crazy heat and congestion of Bangkok, the cool suburban forests and waterfalls, the northern farmland near Chiang Mai, the southern beaches and the islands, the food, and the wonderful, gentle, friendly people—all of that mixed together had helped to make these past six years the best of his life.

He was going to miss all of it when he was gone.

Once the truck hit the paved road, it was a quick ten-minute trip to a small health clinic on the eastern outskirts of town. It was a two-story building painted gray with a large, faded red cross on the side wall. Nattapong rushed inside and returned in less than a minute with a nurse and a gurney. They all helped lift David and push him inside. The nurse and a young Thai doctor wheeled him into a small empty room. Teerapat continued to hold David's arm as the nurse injected a vial of morphine. David's eyes fluttered a moment, then shut.

Bob placed his hand on David's forehead and said a silent prayer for his recovery. It was quiet in the room except for the slow, steady beep of the old heart rate monitor, a large boxy contraption that looked straight out of a 1950s movie. The forest had taken its toll on the young lad, but to Bob it had given crystal-clear vision, an uncluttered mind, the most certain and prescient he had had in weeks. He knew what he had left to do. He patted Nattapong and Teerapat on their shoulders, then said goodbye. He walked out the front of the clinic where the driver of the truck was waiting for him. Bob took out a one thousand Thai baht bill and pressed it in the driver's hand.

"Thanks, mate, but I'll walk."

"Rain," the driver said and pointed to the sky as a steady drizzle continued to fall.

"No worries," Bob said and strolled to the edge of the road.

The first place he came to was a tire shop. Two men were working in a cluttered garage stacking rubber treads in one corner of the room. Bob walked up to them, handed each a one thousand baht bill, smiled, and bowed his head. The two men stared with open mouths, unable to speak before Bob left the shop and kept moving along the road.

Next, Bob saw a middle-aged woman pushing a cart of firewood along the side of the road. He gave her two thousand baht. After her was a small roadside café. Four people were there eating bowls of noodle soup, and two people were working. He gave each of them one thousand baht as well.

A gas station, a pack of teenagers, a machine shop, a bottled water wholesaler, a man with one arm, a daycare center with fifteen children and three teachers—each time Bob stopped to reach into his pocket and pull out paper bills, giving them out with a bowed head and a smile. His white shirt was rain soaked by the time he reached the three pagodas at the center of town. He ventured into the tourist market where tables of souvenirs and wood carvings and T-shirts and postcards lined the narrow alleyway. He gave away another twenty thousand baht there, pulling apart a dozen more upper and lower jaws with surprise.

The sky was nearly dark, and the streetlamps surrounding the three pagodas had started to buzz to life when he began to climb the hill toward Miss Sally's private boarding house. His left pocket was now empty of money, but his right pocket was still stuffed full. The falling rain began to pick up speed.

Chapter Twenty-Five

The boarding house run by Miss Sally was not far from the gates to the refugee camp, just around a bend in the road at the top of the hill. It was nearly invisible in the darkness of the early night sky. There were no lights nearby, and it was painted a deep-brown color that blended in with the forest at its back. The shape reminded Michael of the split-level home he had grown up in; a squat two-story main building was connected to a long one-story extension that had four bedrooms, two on each side.

The teenage waiter from the café, who introduced himself as Jimmy, showed Michael to one of the rooms facing the street. It was clean and simple with a bed and table and sink, and Michael dropped off his backpack, then went into the salon in the main building. The rain was falling harder, and the machine-gun sound of it banging on the tin roof created a wall of noise in the room to go along with all the bustling activity as everyone had a job to do to prepare for their big night. Two other Thai teenagers were in the house as well: a tall, skinny boy with shoulder-length hair was painting two bright orange life jackets a dark-brown color to match the river, while a teenage girl with triple-pierced ears and wearing a Mariah Carey T-shirt was busy cooking pad Thai in the kitchen. Ramanya was sitting on the teak wood floor packing two phone-book-sized, waterproof bags with supplies such as flashlights, batteries, matches, rope, and bags of nuts and dried fruit. Miss Sally entered with a first aid kit and motioned for Michael to sit at the dining table.

She peeled off the blood-soaked ribbon of orange fabric, with some pieces tearing off and getting stuck inside the wound. She removed them with a pair of tweezers, then soaked cotton pads in hydrogen peroxide that sizzled and popped and foamed and burned, and Michael bit down on his shirt collar as lightning first flashed outside the window.

"You'll need to get this stitched up," said Miss Sally as she wrapped a fresh bandage around his arm. "And clean it every day. This is how my husband died. A cut on his leg. It seemed like nothing at first, but it turned septic."

"I will. I'm sorry to hear that. How long ago?"

"Five years now."

"And you have a daughter?"

"Yes. Eleven. And a son, nineteen. He studies at university in Sydney. He wants to be a barrister one day."

"Your accent. Do you mind if I ask how you got that?"

"My father was a diplomat. I spent most my childhood in Hong Kong."

A loud knock at the door and the boy Jimmy looked out the window, then opened it. Father Bob rushed in, his clothes drenched.

"What happened to you?" asked Michael.

Bob looked at the wound on Michael's arm. "I walked. What happened to you?"

"I fell."

Jimmy brought a towel for Bob to begin drying off. "There is a warm kettle in the kitchen," said Miss Sally. "Help yourself to some tea."

"Cheers," Bob said and left the salon.

Miss Sally finished tightening the bandage. "That should hold you until you can get someone proper to look at it."

"Thanks so much."

"My son wants to live in America one day."

Michael smiled. "I'll give you my number and e-mail. He can

look me up, though I live in South Carolina."

"He wants to go to Los Angeles."

"Ugh… I lived there for a year. Not my favorite place."

"I tell him it's not like in the movies."

"No, it definitely isn't."

Another knock at the door and this time Jimmy looked out the window, turned around, and pointed at his chin.

"Your friend is here," said Miss Sally to Ramanya.

Through the doorway walked the man with the scar on his chin. He wore an olive-colored rain poncho and held a plastic bag in his hands. He gave the traditional *wai* greeting to the room as Ramanya stood up and walked over to him. Bob entered the room, holding a hot mug of tea and with the towel draped over his shoulder.

"This is Thura," said Ramanya. "The man who will guide me to my family."

"A nice night for a walk in the woods," Thura said and smiled. He began to take items out of the plastic bag and gave them to Ramanya. "Here… I have a raincoat for you and some clothes to change into."

Bob carefully watched the man as Ramanya unfolded another olive poncho like the one Thura was wearing, as well as a set of dark-blue short pants, black T-shirt, and dark-blue sneakers. "Thank you," Ramanya said. "I'll change when we get to the forest."

"How much are you getting paid for this?" Bob asked the man and sipped his tea.

"Nothing, sir," said Thura. "I am a friend of the family who has been sheltering Pra Ramanya's family. I only hope to be paid with his happiness and perhaps with rewards in my next life."

"Mm," Bob said and looked into the man's eyes. He couldn't find anything disingenuous.

An old rotary wall phone suddenly rang out. Miss Sally crossed the room to pick it up after the first ring. She spoke quickly in Thai then hung up.

"It's starting," she said. "A military truck with extra soldiers is on the way. They will be here within a few hours."

Everyone stopped what they were doing and came into the salon. Miss Sally looked at all of them. "First, I want to thank all of you for the help you have offered here tonight. As some of you know, my husband was from the Mon tribe. We met in Bangkok when we were young, and he was a good man, a hard-working man who came here as a child through these woods to create a better life for himself. We had a few successful shops in Bangkok for many years, but eventually we were pulled here to this border town to do what we could to help others such as himself." She looked at

Ramanya. "Now, we are helping one of our brothers to return to his homeland and be reunited with his family. I understand what a difficult decision it must have been for you, but I also know how powerful are those bonds that keep us together, that keep us strong. That is why I wish you all the fortune possible on your journey tonight, but that is also why I must now go to my home to be with my family as well." She looked at Bob and Michael. "I'll return here in the morning."

"Thank you, Miss Sally," said Bob. "Well said. We will take it from here."

She half smiled and nodded her head. She grabbed Ramanya's hands and pressed them tightly in her own, briefly touched Michael on his arm near his wound, then took an umbrella from a stand near the door, and exited into the dark, wet night.

The teenage girl pointed to the kitchen. "Food now," she said. "Yum. Yum."

Chapter Twenty-Six

The four men—Father Bob, Ramanya, Michael, and Thura—sat in silence in the salon. The entire house was now dark except for a single petrol lantern spreading thick shadows on the cinder-block walls. The teenagers had left soon after dinner. A pink and white analog Hello Kitty wall clock showed the time as 9:57 p.m.

The heavy sound of the rain on the tin roof began to quiet down to a small pattering as the storm outside eased for a moment. Each man breathed in deeply but steadily, over and over, until the cat paw of the minute hand reached the number twelve. In the distance, in between the broken walls of rain, they could now hear a mechanical noise, a low humming and pounding sound, growing louder and closer.

"This is it," Bob said and stood up.

They opened the door and went out to the dark street. From

the top of the hill, they could see a long distance back along the main road, and at the end of the tree line, where the mountains began to rise, they could see a set of blinking lights moving through the sky. Down at the center of town, a large crowd had already gathered, filling the roundabout and the field where the three pagodas stood, their white and gold colors lit up at night.

Bob turned to face Ramanya, placed his hands on his shoulders. "Do you have everything you need?" Ramanya nodded yes. "Ok. I'll go down there and run interference if I see any problems... Good luck, my friend. I will pray for you. I'm sure you will find them, and I'm sure you will live a long and happy life together."

"Thank you, Father Bob. And please thank the others at your ministry."

"I will." Bob looked at Thura. "Take good care of him."

"Yes, sir."

"Michael, I'll see you back here tonight."

"Yes."

The sound of the air being sliced apart grew louder, and they could now see the entire outline of the helicopter moving toward town. The pace of the raindrops began to pick up again.

"Ok," said Bob. "Let's do it."

When they reached the edge of the forest, Ramanya ducked behind a tree and took off his orange robes. He put on the clothes Thura had brought for him and slipped the rain poncho over his body. Behind them the pounding, pounding of the helicopter grew louder as Michael scanned the edge of the dark woods, bouncing his flashlight off trunks until he found the first yellow mark he had left with the can of paint.

"Got it!" he said in a forceful whisper. "Over here." Ramanya and Thura joined him by the tree. "You want me to take those?" asked Michael, motioning to the orange robes in Ramanya's hands.

"No, I will keep them. It doesn't feel right to give them away just yet." He opened the thick waterproof bag he had prepared at the house and pushed them inside, then pulled the strap of the bag over his shoulder. Thura carried the two life jackets on one arm, and all three men took the coil of rope, stretching it out between them as they descended down into the forest...

Father Bob reached the center of town where a crowd of a couple of thousand stood in the rain and looked in the sky as the helicopter grew nearer. Word must have spread quickly to the surrounding villages, and he knew that beyond the excitement factor, there were many people in this part of the country who supported what the rebels had tried to do. The wind blew the umbrella in his hand, and he looked at the streets surrounding the pagodas. Everyone must have come on foot or by bicycle, for he only saw one vehicle, a blue van, parked by itself at the bottom of the hill leading to Miss Sally's.

The wind from the storm was quickly replaced by the cyclone of the helicopter's blades, and the deafening noise devoured the air as the Thai military chopper reached the field and hovered for a moment. The soldiers from the Thai checkpoint left their posts and hurried toward the crowd fighting to stand up straight as the people held onto hats and bags and each other's shoulders until at last the chopper began its descent...

Michael led the way through the forest, past the small mud huts, looking up to see each of the yellow streaks of paint he had left earlier that day. The wet leaves stuck to his legs, and the sounds of the rushing water below them, the helicopter behind them, and the rain above them swirled together into a constant roar. He held the end of the rope that stretched along the nearly invisible path, Ramanya held the rope in the middle, and Thura held it at the end, the three men connected, moving together as one animal, down, down the valley, until at last they came to the large boulders jutting

282

from the earth.

They stopped. Ramanya came up to Michael and took his hand. "This is it, teacher," he said.

Michael's chest heaved up and down, sucking in the cool air. "What?"

"We will go from here. You don't need to climb these rocks again with your arm. Not at night. Not in the rain."

"But... How will I know you made it across?"

"You remember that branch on the opposite side?"

"Yes."

"When we get across, I will hang something on it. You will be able to see it in the morning."

"But..."

Thura reached out and touched Michael's arm. "It's ok, sir. I will make sure he is safe."

Michael continued to breathe in and out, and he looked down at the rock then back at the faces of the two men, the barely seen outlines in the black air. He nodded. "Ok... ok."

Ramanya took Michael's head in both his hands, pressing his palm against each side of his face, the warmth of Ramanya's hands cutting through the rainwater on Michael's skin. He pulled Michael toward him and kissed Michael on his forehead. "Thank you, teacher. For everything."

"Of course... Don't forget to study your English."

Ramanya smiled. "I won't."

And then Ramanya and Thura disappeared down the boulder and into the future of the night...

The blades of the chopper reduced to half speed, and the soldiers from the checkpoint had made their way across the field and were now pushing the crowd back. The side doors opened, and two more soldiers from inside climbed out. The first of the rebels then emerged, a tall thin man in a camouflage jumpsuit, and the crowd erupted in a roaring cheer. The rebel shook his hands above his head before one of the Thai soldiers moved him away from the helicopter door. One by one four more rebels, a mixture of members of the Karen National Liberation Army and the Vigorous Burmese Student Warriors, stepped onto the field and each time the crowd cheered. Finally, the last man—Jonny—stepped out, and the crowd screamed even louder. Jonny smiled and flashed a V for Victory sign, and then he looked across the crowd and saw Bob at the edge of the field. He smiled and nodded at Bob.

Bob dropped his umbrella to the ground and with both hands pulled out the large stacks of Thai money from his pocket. He threw the money in the air where it caught up in the draft from the helicopter blades and flew all over the field, a snowstorm of cash. The crowd went into a frenzy, rushing and stampeding everywhere to grab the bills, pushing toward the chopper as the Thai soldiers frantically blew their whistles, but there was nothing they could do to stop them. The rebels seized on the moment and bolted into the crowd, disappearing into the hurricane of bodies as Bob continued to throw money toward the sky. One of the soldiers grabbed a bullhorn and began shouting at the crowd, but he could barely be heard, sounding like an old frog croaking from behind a wall of glass...

Michael could hear the shouting and cheering from town as he began to climb back up the valley, but then he heard another sound, a sharp, loud voice yelling, "Hey! Hey!"

He looked below him and saw a man with a large bright flashlight walking toward the boulders. He couldn't imagine any of the refugees carrying a light like that, nor would they come this far into the woods. He remembered what Ramanya had said about locals sometimes getting hired to patrol the forest, and Michael dug into his backpack and took out his multi-tool, flipped up the short knife blade, and went back down the hill. As the man reached the top of the rocks, he kept shouting to the passageway below. Michael suddenly stepped in front of him, tripping him to the ground, and fell on top of him.

"Oh! I'm sorry! So sorry!" he said, pressing down on the man as he tried to get up. The man tried to raise his leg and kick Michael off of him, but Michael pressed down harder, used his left hand to grab the man's neck, and then brought the knife blade right up to the edge of the man's eye. The man stopped moving. Michael looked at him and shook his head. "No," he whispered and pressed his hand harder on his neck, touching the blade to the bottom of the man's eyelid. *"Khao jai mai?"* said Michael, looking into his eyes. "Do you understand?"

The man quietly shook his face to indicate yes. Michael waited a moment to be sure, then released his grip from the man's neck and stood up. The man picked up his flashlight and turned it off. Michael gripped the multi-tool in his hand and watched the man brush wet leaves off his body, then turn around, and walk back toward the direction he came. He waited until the man faded into the dark woods, and then a flash of lightning lit up the trees showing them to be empty except for himself. A burst of thunder soon followed, and Michael resumed his climb out of the valley...

The Thai soldiers gave up trying to control the crowd. The pilot of the chopper waved to them to get inside, and the blades clicked and began to spin faster and faster, the rush of wind pushing the crowd back toward the street. As the chopper rose into the air, most people began to walk away, but some still chased a few of the loose bills that floated around the field. Within five minutes the helicopter had disappeared over the horizon, and the roundabout had emptied to less than a dozen people. The rebels were nowhere to be seen. Bob picked up the umbrella and began to walk up the hill to Miss Sally's house. As he crossed in front of the van, the headlights exploded to life, covering Bob in bright white light. Bob stopped walking and the lights stayed on. No one emerged from the van, but Bob knew who they were. The lights burned onto his face, searing his eyes, sending him a clear message: the end game was here.

Bob gave one short, quick wave to the van, then continued up the hill.

Chapter Twenty-Seven

The rain now fell in a torrent, lightning and thunder flashing quicker and more violently as Michael arrived back at Miss Sally's dark boarding house. He shook rainwater back and forth off his body like a wet dog and opened the door to his small bedroom. He found Father Bob inside, sitting on a chair.

"Hey! You scared me! I wasn't expecting you."

Bob stood up. "Did they make it?"

"Yes. I think so. Ramanya didn't want me to go all the way to the river. But, yes, I think, I'm sure they did. What happened in town? We heard a lot of noise... Wow. I really need a beer."

Bob stood next to Michael, looming over him. "Sorry, mate," he said, then raised his right arm and smashed his fist as hard as could against Michael's head.

Michael's knees buckled, and he grabbed onto the edge of the table for support. "Fuck, Bob! What the fuck? What are you doing?"

Bob again smashed his fist against the side of Michael's face. Again, Michael stumbled. A third time he pounded against the lad, then Bob twisted his body and landed a fourth and final violent punch against Michael's head. That one did it, and Michael was knocked unconscious. Thirty years ago, thought Bob, he might have taken him out with one punch.

Bob reached out and grabbed the back of Michael's head as he fell down, keeping his skull from smashing against the concrete floor. Bob took off Michael's shoes, then his wet shirt and pants, and took a towel hanging by the sink and dried his hair and skin as much as he could. He dragged then lifted Michael's body and put him in the small bed. Bob covered him in sheets and blankets, then picked up Michael's backpack, unzipped the front pocket and placed it in the chair. He put a bottle of water on the nightstand next to the bed. Bob pressed his hand on Michael's forehead, patted his cheek, then locked the bedroom from the inside and shut the door.

He could hear the van slowly climbing the dark hill.

Almighty and merciful God... Michael would be fine, but Bob wanted to make sure he was not involved in this final act. When Bob was at university in London, during those years when he left the church, many times at the parties he went to with his classmates, sometimes with Sarah, those raucous, secular, bohemian affairs where they would sit on the floor of someone's flat and drink wine, listen to music, and smoke pot, his classmates often talked about a novel that was wildly popular at the time, called *The Unbearable Lightness of Being.* Bob never read it, but he always liked the title, found it clever and evocative, and today, starting with this morning, when he first woke and the world felt lighter and less heavy, and he knew something felt different, he now thought a slight change in that title, to *The Bearable Lightness of Not Being,* best described this day in his life.

Command thy angels to guide and protect us... That light feeling died momentarily, earlier this morning, outside the travel shop when Manny's goons grabbed and shoved him into that alley. The mobile phone, the demand for an answer. Crooked Teeth, his breath smelling like rotting fish. And when Bob told Manny he could kiss his British arse, he thought it would end right then and there, with Big Guy snapping his neck. But they were just middlemen, hired hands. They weren't the buyers, the true clients willing to pay the bounty on his head. Those were in the blue van now climbing up the hill.

Be our assiduous companions for our journey... That moment outside the travel shop had sealed his fate, and Bob knew it. For the hours that followed on the bus trip, he had wallowed in the death trap he had created. But then everything began to change when they had sat in the forest, and Bob had looked up into the tree and saw the great cat, the leopard. When the trees parted and the sky sent an orb of sunshine to warm his face, it was then that all the weight, all the sadness, all everything disappeared, and the voice he heard in his head was clear and direct: This is my time. This is my day.

Preserve us from all evil and especially from sin and guide us to our heavenly home... Bob walked around the building to his bedroom on the other side. The rain had nearly stopped, but the lightning and thunder continued to increase in speed and intensity. As soon as he entered the room, he took off his wet shirt and put on his black clergy shirt. He knelt on the floor, opened his Bible to Psalms, then put the white clerical collar back around his neck, threading it through the shirt. He took a deep breath and waited.

His legacy. His name. How he would be remembered. It was vanity, yes, he had to admit, but he would not allow those five months with Sarah, as much as he had enjoyed them and found nothing sinful or wrong about them, he would not allow those lost days to taint all he had done, all these years, all the hundreds of thousands of miles he had traveled, all the people whose lives he had intersected and helped, all around the world. He had lived a full and just life. He would keep his good name intact and his secrets buried in the ground.

And he would not get Sarah and the boy involved. They didn't deserve it, and he wouldn't do it. And he would not try to disappear and live somewhere else, living the rest of his life looking over his shoulder at shadows creeping around street corners and alleyways. He had done that the past six weeks, and that had been enough. His whole adult life had been bouncing from place to place and here, in Thailand, these past six years was the closest he had ever come to settling down. The only way he would leave it would be to go to his final home, to at last be united with his Creator.

Forever and ever, Amen... The door to his room burst open and the last image Bob saw before the machete came down on the space between his shoulder and neck was Tommy rushing up on his motorcycle shouting "Bollocks! Bollocks!" a wide grin stretching across the boy's face.

And then *poof!...* just like that... In this world, Father Bob Hanlan ceased to exist.

Part Four

Monday, October 4, 1999

They run in all directions. The helicopter, the crowd, the noise give them invisibility. Three head south of town. They will stay in this country and disappear into the nearby villages. Jonny and the driver run to the border. They slip behind the dark market stalls and watch as the only two soldiers on the Burmese side leave their posts and step across the gates, pulled like a riptide toward the spectacle in the center of town. It's easy. The two men run along shadow lines down the road into Burma. They dive into the forest.

"Are you going to the city?"

"Not yet," says Jonny. "I have something yet to do."

"Be safe then."

"Good travels, brother. I will see you soon."

Jonny moves forward alone. Past creeks and abandoned pathways, past a field of cassava to a small shed sitting along the edge. His silver watch shows just past midnight. Plenty of time. Inside the shed is a bag of clothes. He pulls out a jacket with brass buttons that catch a glimpse of the faint moonlight…

Chapter Twenty-Eight

Michael awoke to someone shaking his arm. His eyelids cracked open, and the first burst of light sent a sharp bolt of pain to his head. It throbbed and felt as if it had been filled with concrete. He couldn't lift it from the pillow and just stared at the wall in front of him. Someone shook his arm again.

"Mister Shaw," he heard Miss Sally's voice say. "Michael, you need to get up. I need to get you out of here."

A wave of nausea swirled in his stomach and throat as he tried to sit up in the bed. Miss Sally wrapped her arms around his chest and helped tilt him upright. Michael grabbed his head with both hands, feeling like a hot piece of steel had been jammed into his brain.

"What time is it?" Michael said, slurring some of his words.

"Just past first light."

Michael glanced at the window, then looked at the table that sat at a crooked angle.

"Bob… He hit me."

"He was trying to protect you."

"Where is he?"

"You need to get dressed. You need to get out of here. The police are on the way."

"Police?"

"Please. Put on some clothes and come outside. I'll get some aspirin for your head." Miss Sally left the room.

He moved like he was floating in zero gravity. Michael pulled on the last set of dry clothes he had, a blue T-shirt and khakis. Each step sent a sizzling stream of heat to his skull, and the left side of his face ached. He saw a quick glimpse in the mirror over the sink, the purple and black swath of bruising covering the skin between his cheek and eye. He pushed his wet clothes and the rest of his belongings into the backpack then went outside, expecting the sunlight to increase the pain, but was relieved somewhat to find a cloudy sky. Miss Sally was waiting for him.

"Where's Bob?" he asked again. Miss Sally just stared back at him, her light-brown eyes searching for what to say. Michael began to walk to the other side of the building. "What's going on?"

"Michael, please—"

But Michael ignored her and turned the corner to Bob's room. The first swath of blood ran from the doorway across the concrete walkway to the nearby patch of grass, the tips of which were stained dark red. Michael looked at the door itself, and there, pinned to the wood with a switchblade, was Bob's white clerical collar, but it was not white anymore, it too was bathed in blood. Everything he saw was surreal, like he was watching it on television, and he watched himself push open the door, to see the walls and floors covered in puddles, in streaks, in splatters of blood. The furniture remained, but that was it. There was no body and none of Bob's belongings.

Michael ran out the room, and the whole inside of his body exploded and came rushing out his mouth in a violent, acidic stream. Gasping for breath, he couldn't stop choking, and he sunk to his knees in the red-tipped grass. Miss Sally knelt beside him, holding him around the waist and running her other hand over and over his shoulder and neck.

"He's gone," she whispered. "There is nothing you can do... He's gone. He's gone. He's gone... There is nothing you can do."

"Who... Why?"

"From the other side. The junta was behind it."

"He said he was in trouble but I didn't know. I didn't know it was this bad… He knew this was going to happen?"

"I think so. Yes."

"Did you?"

"No. He didn't tell me anything."

Miss Sally helped Michael stand up. "We need to get you out of here. The military on the Burmese side continued arriving just after midnight. More are on the way. They are very angry about what happened last night. The Thai military is coming up the road. Things could get very ugly. Fast."

"The river," said Michael.

"Come on. Let's go."

"Wait. I have to go down to the river for a moment. I need to see something."

"Hurry. I'll be at my café in town."

His body sore, his head still pounding, Michael climbed as fast as he could up the hill to the refugee camp. The light and the pain burned his eyes, eyes that filled with water as he found the first yellow mark and stumbled into the forest. He moved down the slope with the images of blood swirling in his head: the bloody room, the bloody collar—blood, blood, blood, blood—blood on his arm, dried blood on his face as he leapt over the boulders, and down the passageway to the edge of the river.

And there it was: across the water on the other side, stuck to the large branch were Ramanya's orange robes, the robes he wore when Michael first met him. They moved like a flag in the early morning breeze, a final goodbye, a signal, a sign of success. At first that was all Michael saw, and then he noticed the line of Myanmar soldiers spreading along the riverbank on the other side, and a truck lumbered down one of the dark-green hills where soldiers emerged carrying steel poles and coils of wire. One of the soldiers looked up and saw the robes, then tore them down, shredding them and tossing them in the water where they began to float away. The soldier looked across the river directly at Michael, and Michael wondered: *were you there last night, was it you who came in the room, or do you know who did, are you friends, did you laugh about it this morning, the killing of the priest?*

Chapter Twenty-Nine

He hadn't worn shoes in sixteen months, so the back of the canvas
sneakers Thura had given Ramanya were cutting into the skin just
above his heels. They sat in a thicket of wild indigo bushes, hidden
from sight, looking across a short field to a military outpost. Behind
an L-shaped bend of fences topped with swirls of barbed wire were
three tin-roofed, low-slung buildings and an open garage containing
two large cargo trucks. A single soldier stood on the outside of the
fence near the front gate and smoked a cigarette. It was a small post,
but there was no way to travel around it. Behind it, two large hills
rose into the sky, the crest of one in the shape of an eagle's beak.
Behind *those* hills, Thura had told Ramanya, were two more
mountains, and halfway up the second one, in a patch of forest with
no roads and with no visitors, including the government soldiers, was
where Ramanya's mother and sister were waiting for him.

They had crossed the river last night without much incident. They could hear all the shouting and noise from the center of town as they held the rope between them, pressed their free arms on the life jackets, and tiptoed across the river bottom. In only a few places did the current lift their feet for a moment and threaten to push them off course. Once across, Ramanya had taken his orange robe and hung it on the tree branch, and then they had moved swiftly away from the riverbank and into the hills of Burma. After three hours of walking, they had stopped to rest and snack on the nuts and dried fruit they had packed at Miss Sally's house. The air smelled like home. It was different from Thailand, where there always seemed to be a sweetness tinged to the air, but back in Burma it was more earthen— a deep scent of red dirt and wet bark.

Several soldiers now spilled into the courtyard of the post and began to move pallets of equipment and load them into the trucks.

"Almost," whispered Thura. "Almost."

"Are you certain?"

"Yes."

They had arrived just at first light and had been waiting for nearly two hours since. Ramanya took out two pieces of the sweet *jaggery* candy and handed one to Thura. The sugar dissolved on his tongue, leaving behind a slightly tart flavor of tamarind.

Behind them, a long-tailed shrike called out from the top of the canopy; as if in response to that, from behind the fence, a soldier blew a sharp whistle three times in a row, and the two trucks roared to life. All the others scrambled out of the barracks and climbed inside the back of the trucks, and the soldier on the outside pulled apart both sides of the gates. The ground beneath their feet vibrated as the trucks moved down the sloped road, around a curve, and disappeared between two narrow rock walls. They were heading toward the border.

Everything grew silent again, and the one single soldier remained on the outside of the gate. He appeared to be looking across the field where Ramanya and Thura were hiding. He stood motionless for several moments. Then he slowly began to walk toward them.

Ramanya clamped down on his back teeth. He looked at Thura with eyes wide in disbelief. Tissa had been right; this whole thing had been a trap. The soldier grew closer and closer, and Ramanya looked around for a place to dash into the forest… But Thura reached out and gently placed his hand on Ramanya's tensed forearm. "It's ok," he whispered. "It's ok."

The soldier reached the bushes, the brass buttons of his gray jacket catching bolts of the morning sun. He squatted down and pulled back one of the branches to see the two men. He took off his cap, to reveal a decidedly flattened, slick black pompadour. He pressed his hands in front of his face, closed his eyes, and bowed his head.

"Pra Ramanya," Jonny said. "It is an honor to meet you."

Ramanya exhaled, the hot river of tension covering his whole body suddenly fading away. "I'm not a monk anymore."

"But you will always be our brother," the man said.

"This is Jonny," Thura said. "He was the man who led the demonstration at the embassy."

"But—" Ramanya said, then stopped.

"Yes," Jonny said. "You weren't the only reason we did it, but we had hoped one outcome would be to create a distraction so we could bring you back. To your country. To your family." He turned and pointed at the eagle-beak mountain. "They are waiting for you. They are not far away."

Jonny took off the military jacket and threw it and the cap into the forest, leaving only his undershirt. He then reached in and took Ramanya's hand to help pull him to his feet. "Come," he said. "Let's finish this."

Chapter Thirty

Michael left the riverbank behind, and up, up, up the valley one last time he went until he was back on the paved road heading toward town. He could see down to the roundabout, now filling with jeeps and trucks and soldiers from the Thai military. The air was crisp and cool, and the throbbing in his head began to fade away. He came to the café and found Miss Sally standing alone by the kitchen door.

"Could I have a beer, please?"

"I'll join you," she said and brought two bottles and two frosted glasses on a tray.

They sat in silence for a while slowly sipping the beer. Michael could see the Thai soldiers putting up steel gates and fences on this side to match the steel gates and fences being built on the Myanmar side. He looked at Miss Sally, and without speaking, she could hear the question in his eyes.

"I don't know," she said. "I know what happened to him in Beirut, and I know he would never let himself be a prisoner again. I don't know exactly what kind of trouble he was in now, but it had to be profound. I also know he wouldn't want to run away… A life lived in hiding is not much of a life at all."

A woman from the street came to the edge of the patio and motioned to Miss Sally. "Excuse me," Miss Sally said and stood up. "I have to take care of something."

Michael lit a cigarette and continued to watch the soldiers move and build and whistle and shout, and then suddenly everything grew completely silent in his mind. He could see all the activity, but he had pressed the mute button on the world. Cool air swirled around his head, and then the image came to him as if beamed down via satellite directly into his brain: he could see Ramanya walking up a hill into a village, and he could see a woman and a young girl emerge from a small house, and he could see them embrace, could see their arms trembling and hear their breaths and their sobs of joy.

The world around him came back on, and he again heard the soldiers blowing their whistles. He then looked at his backpack at his feet and saw an unexpected flash of bright blue from inside the front pocket. He pulled out a bright-blue envelope with the name Siam

Travel stamped on the front. In the envelope he saw money; he counted ten thousand Thai baht. Behind it he pulled out two pieces of paper. The first was a note with Bob's handwriting. It said: Remember: No matter where you go, there you are. The other piece of paper was a plane ticket, open-ended, paid in full, one way from Bangkok to Columbia, South Carolina.

The breeze lifted the large leaves of the banana trees that circled the street. Michael put out his cigarette and sat, moment after moment after moment, looking at Bob's final gift. There was only one way to thank him.

Sorry, Sherri, but I can't come to dinner with you and your mother next week. Sorry, secretaries, bowling sounds wonderful, but not next week. Sorry Tissa. Sorry Nanda and all the others at Wat Prok, no more grammar, no more vocabulary for a while. You will have to study on your own. And Kat, Miss Kitty Kat, our kiss, our tenuous possibility, and our trip to Ayutthaya; I'm sorry but it will have to wait. Probably a very long time. "Next week" will probably never come.

Miss Sally came back to the patio.

"Hey, I'm going to need a driver," Michael said.

"Certainly. To Bangkok?"

Michael stood up, finished his glass of beer, and slammed it on the table. He stared at it, watching the last streak of foam slide to the bottom and break apart. He looked up at the one single road leading away from the center of town. He took in a deep breath.

"Yes. To the airport… It's time to go home."

Chapter Thirty-One

For two more hours, they climbed through thick forest brush, and the land was silent, and they were silent, only the occasional blast of song from restless birds acknowledging their presence. Finally, as they came about three-quarters of the way up the last mountain, the forest gave way to a small circular clearing. Four houses, built with red mud and thatched roofs stretched along the far side. The three men stopped. Ramanya's lip began to quiver and he looked at Thura. Thura smiled and silently nodded, then put two fingers in his mouth, and gave two quick bursts of call. The doors to three of the houses opened, and two teenage boys, an elderly man with a cane, and three women in their twenties emerged, wearing faded clothes and dusty fabric wrapped around their waists. One of the teenage boys knocked on the door of the farthest home.

An eleven-year-old girl with a pink barrette in her hair poked her head out then froze for a moment. Ramanya stared at her, at first not recognizing his sister because of how tall she had grown. The girl suddenly bolted from the house and ran across the field, leaping her skinny legs in the air and wrapping them around Ramanya's body. Ramanya held her as tight as he could without choking the air from her chest.

"Marli," Ramanya whispered. "How big you are now. I can hardly hold you."

"I knew you'd come back," she said and buried her nose into Ramanya's neck.

He lifted her over his head, kissed her cheek, then put her back on her feet. "Where is she? Can she move? How bad is she?"

The young girl smiled and pointed to the house. There, a middle-aged woman, her black hair carefully folded into a bun, wearing a long red skirt with yellow painted flowers, emerged and walked across the courtyard. She smiled, her eyes glistening, her hands spread open in front of her chest. Ramanya took several steps forward and met her. She took his face in her hands and pressed her forehead against his. Ramanya's shoulders heaved up and down as water rolled from his eyes.

"Ramanya," she simply whispered.

"Mother," Ramanya sighed out. "I didn't know—"

"I know," she said and stopped him.

"How bad are you? Is it getting worse?"

His mother continued to smile, then gently slapped his face. "I'm fine. There is nothing wrong." She looked over to Thura and nodded her head. "I just wanted to make sure you came back." She gave him a big hug, and Ramanya breathed in, smelling the lilac scent of her skin that he had always known.

Thura and Jonny went over to one of the side houses and sat down in chairs away from the courtyard, giving the family space.

"Tissa did not come," Ramanya said.

"He is good where he is. He has no one here anymore. His uncle passed last year…" She and Marli took each of Ramanya's hands and led him to their small house. "Come. I made some soup for you. All bones is what being a monk has turned you into."

The three paused a moment in the doorway. Ramanya looked back at Thura and Jonny. They each closed their eyes and bowed their heads.

"Come inside," said Marli. Ramanya entered the three-room hut. The smell of curry soup drifted from a black pot that simmered over a small fireplace. Ramanya took off his shoes and dug his feet in the cool dirt floor, using his toes to spread the dirt as a soothing balm across the cuts in his heels. His mother pulled a wooden chair to the center of the room, and Ramanya let his body tumble and collapse. He saw a white cat lounging in the corner of the main room.

His mother wrapped her arms around his shoulders and gave him a long kiss on his cheek.

"Welcome home."

END

ABOUT THE AUTHOR

RUSH LEAMING lives in the Southeastern United States. He has done many things and lived in many places.

At various times in his life he has been a/an: car wash attendant, bartender, dishwasher, Adjunct Professor, lab rat decapitator, shoe salesman, fish pond builder, film actor (a very poor one), music video director, refugee camp volunteer, film production manager, ESL teacher, star of a country music video, newspaper delivery person, Chinese wok assembler, night time hotel desk clerk, cement mixer, ballet manager, waiter, internet teacher, screenwriter, short film director, Cuban cigar mule, auctioneer, pre-med student, traffic pattern analyzer, photographer, landscaper, homeless, Academic Director, shepherd, lifeguard, audio-visual coordinator, recruiter for a prestigious government agency, and single dad.

Just to name a few...

You can reach him at: www.rushleaming.com